PRAISE FOR BRENDA FELBER

"The Pameroy mysteries never disappoint! I love how history gets mixed into the present. After reading this book, I really feel like I know Lillia and her Grauntie. Great read. Can't wait for the next!"

"The Pameroy Mystery Series is such fun reading! I never figure out the ending until the last page. I can't wait to see what paranormal adventures will come next for Lillia and Grauntie!"

"What a fun mystery! I feel like I am right there with Lillia and Charlie during their adventures. Humorous, lighthearted and quite a page turner! I will definitely be recommending this one every chance I get!"

"Drawn into this book right from the beginning! My thirteen-year-old niece has read both books in this series and loved them. So, it's been nice that we've both enjoyed and can chat about them! Great read not just for tweens."

WHISPERING GRAVES

A PAMEROY MYSTERY IN MASSACHUSETTS

BRENDA FELBER

Cover design-eBook Launch

Publisher-Laughing Deer Press

Publisher's Cataloging-in-Publication data

Names: Felber, Brenda, author.

Title: Whispering Graves : a Pameroy mystery / Brenda Felber.

Series: Pameroy mystery.

Description: Schofield, WI: Laughing Deer Press, 2018.

Identifiers: ISBN 978-1-948064-03-3 (pbk.) | 978-1-948064-04-0 (ebook)

Summary: Lillia Pameroy uses her paranormal powers to help find the missing pieces of a three-hundred-year old silver vanity set crafted by Paul Revere

Subjects: LCSH Massachusetts—History—Revolution, 1775-1783 --
Fiction. | United States—History—Revolution, 1775-1783--Fiction. |
Alcott family--History--Fiction. | Psychics--Juvenile fiction. |
Silverwork--Colonial--Fiction. | Friendship--Fiction. | Ghosts--Juvenile
fiction. | Ghost stories. | Mystery fiction. | Supernatural--Fiction. |
BISAC JUVENILE FICTION / Mysteries & Detective Stories |
JUVENILE FICTION / Horror & Ghost Stories | JUVENILE
FICTION / Paranormal, Occult & Supernatural | JUVENILE
FICTION / Historical / United States / 20th Century

Classification: LCC PZ7.F33375 Wh 2018 | DDC [Fic]--dc23

CONTENTS

QUOTE TO PONDER...

"I'm not afraid of storms, for I'm learning how to sail my ship."

Louisa May Alcott

1

LILLIA

Hiding the strange things that happen to me has been part of my growing up ever since I was four years old. That was when Mom first realized I was different. My imaginings frightened her then, and eight years later, still do.

To be honest, I'm not sure if she is afraid of me or afraid of what she doesn't understand. Either way it hurts.

I love to take trips with my grandaunt Nora. I call her Grauntie. She's not afraid of me or my imagining ability. She gets it. Her brother, my grandpa, was like me. Before he died Grandpa told me to keep an open mind. I try to.

This trip I'm on a ghost scouting mission for my friend Tiffany. She owns a ghost tour business and asked me to check out the spirits in Concord, Massachusetts. She trusts my instincts.

My little brother Charlie is along with us. Charlie studied the American Revolutionary War in his fourth-grade class this year. On our flight to Boston two days ago he couldn't sit still because he would be seeing Boston Harbor where the Boston Tea Party took place. He is crazy for history.

Today we drove on the road British soldiers took to confront the rebellious colonists.

"Many of these houses were here in the 1700s. Imagine people peering out from behind those curtains to watch the British march by," Grauntie said.

"I wish I could have seen Paul Revere galloping on his horse shouting out that the British are coming!" Charlie said.

We are headed to Concord, but it's taking a very long time because Charlie has his mind set on stopping at every one of those roadside historical sites! We watched a movie at the Minute Man Visitor Center, then drove to the Paul Revere Capture Site. And then on to the Captain William Smith house.

I get it. Seeing these places is fine, but we'd only be here a few days. You could spend a month in Massachusetts and not see it all.

It was after we left the Hartwell Tavern that Grauntie said, "Charlie, that's it for the stopping. Mandy Conner is expecting us, and I don't want to be late."

It relieved me to hear that.

Charlie found what he was looking for.

Would I?

2

ENTERING CONCORD

Concord is nestled among the wooded hills of Massachusetts. The waters of the Assabet and Sudbury Rivers join to form the Concord River. The Concord then meanders north to meet with the Merrimack. Together, they flow out to the Atlantic Ocean.

People gather on the banks of the rivers to fish. Or they refresh themselves in watery coolness on a hot sticky summer day. Some locals board small row boats and drift without purpose.

In autumn, the dense hardwoods of Massachusetts flounce about, dressed in deep reds, burning oranges, and vivid yellows. Tourists from across America travel to witness this beauty.

Entering Concord on Lexington Road, Grauntie Nora found herself distracted by another offering of

Concord, the beautiful historic homes lining the roadway. Her head swiveled from side to side trying to read the signs and catch glimpses of the houses.

At one-point Charlie had to shout, "Watch out!"

Nora hit the brakes. Tourist traffic on the two-lane street had slowed.

"Sorry kids, I'll pay attention to the road. I'm just so excited to see these places. That was the Wayside Home we passed, parts of it are three hundred years old. Oh, and look. The Orchard House!"

"Doesn't look very inviting," Charlie said as he took in the somber home. The only pretty thing was the big trees surrounding it and the fall flowers and pumpkins put on the walkway to it.

"That was the style at one time," Nora said. "I agree though, the dark clapboard siding is stark. Louisa May Alcott wrote Little Women in that house. Did you read that novel Lillia?"

"No but I saw the movie a few years ago. About sisters, right? The house in the movie looked just like this one."

Grauntie Nora said, "I think the movie was filmed here. The book was fiction, but Louisa May based much of it on the Alcott sisters and the life they lived here," Grauntie Nora said. "I know that's one place I want to visit while we're here."

Charlie hoped Grauntie wouldn't expect him to go along. He was only interested in seeing the American Revolutionary War sites he'd learned about in history class. So much of it happened right here. He rolled down his window to feel the cool fall air rush by.

Grauntie pointed toward a large white house with black shutters edging the windows. "Look at that will you? It's Ralph Waldo Emerson's house. This is amazing!"

"Easy Grauntie," Lillia laughed. "We have five days here. Don't overheat in the first ten minutes."

When Charlie asked the infamous, "Are we almost there?" Lillia and Grauntie both groaned.

"Yes, Charlie we are almost there." Grauntie made a turn on to Main Street. "Can you guys watch for Main Street Antiques? Mandy told me it has a reddish awning." She stopped the car at a crosswalk, her hands resting on the steering wheel, and a smile on her face. "Ah, just what I pictured a fall street scene in a little New England town would look like."

She took in the fall colors scattered in woven baskets filled with orange, gold and ruby mums. Tall dried stalks of corn were tied to lampposts with bright orange ribbons. More pumpkins and gourds lay scattered among the shop window displays. Rocking chairs and benches encouraged strollers to sit and enjoy the afternoon.

"There it is," Charlie said, pointing at a low brownstone building with a red awning. A vintage wooden sign hung above the front door, proudly proclaiming that this was the Main Street Antique Store.

Nora found a parking space and soon the three travelers were walking along the Main Street of Concord. Smells of hot apple cider, fall leaves, caramel apples, and dry corn greeted them. Smiles from passing strangers welcomed them. And that special cool crispness of a New England fall day enveloped them.

3

LILLIA

Pushing open the door, I heard the welcoming jingle of a bell. The scarred wooden floor creaked as I stepped out of the bright sunshine and into the dim interior of the store.

Taking a deep breath, I soaked in the smells of old dust, dry oiled woods and musty fabrics. Cinnamon and cedar smells rose from the potpourri bowl resting on the table ahead of me.

The store had a pleasing cluttered feeling. Sunshine sneaking under the outside awning bounced off a cut crystal vase collection sending rainbow glimmers through the air. The spillover from displays on tables and chests threatened to block the narrow aisles.

Grauntie was writing in a leather-bound journal next to a sign reading *We love our visitors. Please sign in!* "We might be the only visitors from Kansas signed in here," she said before turning to look for Mandy, the person Tiffany put us in touch with.

A young woman clerk talked in a low voice as she opened the glass front of a dark wood cabinet to pull out a figurine for her customer to see. She carefully reached over a set of gold edged tea cups and a white porcelain dog to reach it.

The other clerk, a plump woman with gray hair pulled in a loose bun at the nape of her neck, nodded eagerly at something a customer was saying.

"Grauntie, is it okay if I wander around?" I asked.

"Be careful though. Don't knock anything over." She turned to look at Charlie. "You want to check the store out too?"

"I'm good right here," Charlie said as he sat on a small wooden bench. "Do you think it's okay to sit on this? It doesn't look too sturdy."

"You may sit there young man," the plump clerk said as she walked up with her customer. "I'm Helen and I'll be right with you soon as I'm done ringing up this purchase."

Objects pulled at me. With tunnel vision, I walked toward a cradle at the turn of the aisle. In it sat a well-loved stuffed bunny. A quilt done in soft pastels hung on the cradle's railing. I heard the soft cry of a baby. The cradle slowly rocked. Back and forth. Back and forth. The crying continued.

From around the bend in the aisle I heard mellow gongs coming from a tall grandfather clock. Next to the clock stood a metal umbrella holder. Against it rested an open umbrella dripping water on the floor. No one was near.

On the wall behind the grandfather clock hung a glass covered painting in an ornate frame. In the glass I saw my reflection and that of someone reaching into the cradle. I didn't turn to look at her because she wasn't really there. I knew she was one of my imaginings. The crying stopped.

A sudden rattling sound startled me. Had I bumped into something?

Then I saw that the curved glass door of a tall lacquered wood cabinet trembled, as though someone was trying to open it. Inside, on the cabinet shelves, silver pieces vibrated.

One of them caught my eye. Elegant curlicues and scrolls surrounded an ornate letter P on the surface of the silver piece.

"Is there something I can help you with?" the young clerk asked. The rattling door stilled. The vibrating stopped.

"Isn't that mirror beautiful? Here, let me get it out for

you." She opened the glass door and took out the mirror. The clerk pointed out it was an original Paul Revere piece and was probably part of a vanity set crafted for someone. "Here, you can look at it."

I took the hand mirror from her.

"The dark mottled spotting on it is just tarnish. We usually leave pieces *as is* when we receive them."

I ran my fingers over the silver work on the back of the mirror before turning it to look in the mirror's face. My hand shook. I took hold of the mirror's edge with my other hand to steady it. The mirror was heavy, but it wasn't weight that caused my trembling, it was what I saw in the mirror.

I couldn't pull my eyes away. I saw the face of a young woman wearing a bridal veil. Her face changed. Like the trick on the internet when faces merge, morphing from one into another and then another. She morphed into a woman crying. Then she appeared holding a child. A fast progression of images flew past. Graying hair. Red plaid cloak. Summer straw hat. She grew older and older...all in the matter of a few seconds.

"Are you all right?"

I looked up at the clerk. I took a deep breath before returning her smile. "Yes, this mirror sure is beautiful. P is the initial of my last name."

The jingling at the front door caught my attention.

The short woman who entered saw Grauntie and hurried over to her. That must be the Mandy.

Grauntie waved me over. I returned the mirror to the clerk who carefully placed it back in the display.

I was excited about the possibilities here for more ghostly encounters. An imagining in the first five minutes!

Looks like I found what I was looking for in this quiet little town of Concord, Massachusetts.

4

GETTING SETTLED

The woman extended her hand to Grauntie Nora. "Sorry I'm so late. I'm Mandy Conner. Welcome to Concord."

"Thank you. I'm Nora Pameroy. I adore your store!"

"I appreciate that. This shop is my passion." Mandy pointed to the tallest girl. "This is my oldest Meg. She has to hurry along to her job right now though."

Meg smiled. "I'll be seeing more of you I'm sure. Catch you later Mom." She gave Mandy a peck on the cheek and ran out.

"And this is my youngest Beth," Mandy said, putting her arm around her daughter. "I was thinking she might enjoy showing Charlie around. I think you've borrowed a bike for him right hon?"

Beth nodded.

Nora said, "That sounds wonderful. Charlie doesn't

always like doing the same things his old grandaunt does."

"There's a bike path out to the North Bridge." Beth said. "There's a whole historic park we can go to Charlie."

Charlie liked what he was hearing. "Is it about the history of the Revolutionary War?"

"Yep it is," Beth answered.

"Okay, sounds like that will work," Mandy said. "Nora, Tiffany mentioned she wanted Lillia to scout out our little town for a possible ghost tour. That's exciting!"

Grauntie Nora said, "Lillia and Tiffany kind of hit it off in San Antonio. And when she mentioned coming here, I jumped at the chance. I can't wait to visit Walden Pond, Orchard House, the Old Manse..."

Mandy smiled. "You're a woman after my own blood Nora Pameroy. Did you notice anything strange about my daughter's names? Oops I missed one. Jo?" Mandy turned, looking for her third daughter. "Jo honey, come here. I want to introduce you to our visitors."

Jo, a tall girl dressed in blue jeans and a plaid flannel shirt, came forward.

"This is my middle daughter Jo."

Grauntie's eyes flashed recognition. "Are your daughters named after the sisters in Little Women? I love it! But wait there's one more. What was her name again?"

Lillia had joined the group and said, "Wasn't it Amy? She was the youngest."

Mandy said, "That's right. After Beth was born, Nate and I decided not to have more children. So, we got a dog for the girls..."

"...and you named her Amy?" Lillia exclaimed.

Mandy laughed. "You catch on quick. Louisa May Alcott wrote Little Women in the Orchard House. You might have driven by it on your way in. Jo here is my writer, just like the character in the book. She has stories published in our town paper."

"Mom, it's no big deal," Jo said, ducking her eyes.

"Nonsense sweetie. I'm proud of you. You have a great imagination."

"Come on Beth and Jo, let's take these guys to their home away from home and let them get settled in," Mandy said.

She told the clerks she would check in with them later and suggested Nora follow in her own car. "Your guest quarters are on a nice quiet street. I hope you like it. The neighborhood is family oriented."

Large trees lined Mill Street. Dogs and children played in piles of leaves. Barks and laughter echoed across the neighborhood. Wide front porches displayed carved pumpkins.

But on the lawn of the house Mandy stopped at the

leaves lay scattered across a dead lawn. The place was eerily quiet as everyone got out of their cars.

The harsh New England climate had worn and weathered the two-story house's dark boards. No light shown in any of the windows. The contrast of its stark bareness was chilling.

"Here you go," Mandy said. "The Peabody house. Isn't it welcoming?"

Nora stared. Unsure what to say. She couldn't help but remember how scared Charlie was with old houses like this. This place looked abandoned.

Beth giggled just as Mandy said, "Okay, enough teasing. This is a place my husband owns. He has big plans for it, but typical of him, it's not as far along as he'd like."

Mandy's snide change of tone made Beth and Jo look awkwardly at each other before reaching to help carry the Pameroy's luggage.

They started down a narrow drive toward the back of the house where another small building sat. Mandy said, "At least Nate got this carriage house cleaned up. He fixed up the small upstairs apartment. Occasionally we rent it out, but with that eyesore in front we haven't had many people staying. And I don't blame them."

Mandy climbed the outside staircase of the carriage house up to its small deck. She pointed out across the yard saying, "We live just down the street. And the famous Sleepy Hollow Cemetery is beyond that swampy area."

Charlie stopped on the stairs and Beth ran into him. "Sleepy Hollow? Like the headless horseman Sleepy Hollow?"

Beth said, "No headless horseman stuff here. That place is a small town in New York. This is our own Sleepy Hollow Cemetery. It's full of plain old everyday dead people. No mysterious or creepy or scary stories."

"It also has lots of famous authors buried in there," Grauntie Nora said to Charlie.

"There's a path that leaves from the back yard and ends up at the cemetery," Mandy said. "The living space above here was probably for the stable hand who took care of the owner's carriage horses. It was in rough shape when we bought the property. Nate added plumbing and electrical so he could have a workshop downstairs."

Mandy tilted her head in the house's direction. "Wish he'd figured out what he wants to do with that old monstrosity."

Inside the apartment was warm and cozy. A blue sofa and arm chair with an ottoman sat near a large window that overlooked the forest behind the house. An antique wooden dining table set sat under a simple glass light fixture in the center of the open space. White kitchen cabinets surrounded a granite topped island.

"That opens up as a sofa sleeper and an air mattress is in the closet. Through that door is the bedroom and the bath," Mandy said. She directed the girls to put the luggage in the bedroom. "I've stocked a few groceries for you. I'm hoping we can meet tomorrow and discuss your plans for the day."

"Thank you so much for accommodating us like this. It's very generous of you," Nora said.

Charlie's mind was stuck on the fact that there was a direct path to a cemetery right outside where they were staying. And an old creepy house next to it.

5

LILLIA

After dinner we went for a walk around our new neighborhood. We headed down the narrow drive that ran past the empty house.

My eyes were still adjusting to the darkness when I heard a strange rustling in the overgrown shrubs.

A black cat screeched and raced across in front of us.

Charlie yelped. "Holy cow, that thing was flying."

Grauntie patted her chest. "That got my old ticker going. A black cat crossing our path...very Halloweenish! We should have brought a flashlight."

I could tell Charlie was glad when we got to the sidewalk. I wrapped my arms around myself. "Flashlight next time sounds like a good plan," I said.

"Hey, Halloween is only a couple days away, right? Are we going to trick-or-treat here?" Charlie asked.

"I don't see why not," Grauntie said.

The neighborhood was quiet now. Children and dogs called in for the evening. Lucky for us that the moon gave light because the only street lamps were on the corners. We'd gone a short distance when Grauntie pointed across the street. "Why that looks like Jo sitting there."

It was Jo. She sat on the porch swing of a pale yellow house. Soft lighting in the porch ceiling made it look like she was on a stage, isolated from us standing in the dark night air.

Charlie gave a whistle. Jo's head jerked up, but it took a minute for her to see the three of us. "Hi!" she said with a big smile. "Come on over."

We walked across the street and up the wide porch stairs. Mums, cornstalks, and carved pumpkins decorated the porch. Fake spiderwebs stretched between the railings. A few big black plastic spiders dangled in the air, attached to strings thumbtacked in the porch ceiling.

Beth came bounding out the front door, followed by a big curly haired dog pushing past her. "Hey guys. Whatcha doing here?"

The dog investigated me. Jo put down the notebook she had been writing in and said, "It's okay, you can pet her."

So I did. Amy wiggled as I scratched behind her ears. "She's the color of my dog." I missed Tucker when we traveled. He was the only one who seemed happy to see me when I got back home. His tail wagging and butt wiggling just like Amy's was doing now.

"We were out for a stroll Beth. This is such a pretty neighborhood," Grauntie said.

Beth leaned back in the door and yelled, "Mom! We have visitors."

Mandy came out, wiping her hands on a kitchen towel. "Well hello there. Exploring the area?"

Beth raced past me and down the porch steps. "Charlie, come on, I'll show you the bike I borrowed for you to use."

Grauntie almost got run over as Charlie followed Beth down and around the corner of the house.

"You home is lovely. So inviting with all the Halloween decorations."

"Thanks Nora. I think autumn is my favorite season." Mandy looked up as an old pickup truck pulled in front of the house. "There's my husband now."

I turned to see Meg climb out of the truck.

Mandy called to her, "Ask Dad to get out for a second, I want him to meet the Pameroys."

A bearded man in a well-worn leather jacket stepped out. He smiled at us as he walked up the front sidewalk with Meg.

"Hi Mom, sorry we missed dinner. I had to stay a

little longer at work. One of the night staff showed up late."

Mandy said. "I left a plate for you in the refrigerator."

Nate walked up. He gave Mandy a quick kiss then turned to me and said, "You must be the gal my sister told me about. Lillia right?" His smile was so warm and welcoming. "Did she show you a good time in Boston?"

"She sure did. That was so nice of her. I loved the harbor area and all the old sailing ships."

"Good to hear. She loves to play tour guide. Maybe she should join her friend Tiffany with the ghost tours."

Mandy said, "Nate, this is Lillia's grandaunt Nora. This is my husband Nate."

"Nice to meet you ma'am," Nate said just as Beth and Charlie came running back to the front of the house. "And this must be Charlie."

Charlie shook Nate's hand. "Nice to meet you, Mr. Conner."

I rolled my eyes. Charlie could be so dorky sometimes. Acting like he's all grown up.

"Beth said she would show me some places tomorrow because I like American Revolutionary War history."

"You two be careful. If you take bikes, be sure to stay on the trails. Fall tourists are still in full force around here and they pay more attention to colored leaves than the road sometimes."

Grauntie let out a low groan. "I'm afraid my tourist genes showed up earlier today. I tried to read too many signs on all the historic homes you have here and Charlie called me out on it."

Nate laughed. "Glad to hear he was paying attention. Hope you enjoy your visit here in Concord. Mandy, I've got a couple more hours of work. I'll reheat my dinner when I get in." He gave Mandy a quick hug and drove off.

"That may be the last you see of him," Mandy said. I think no one missed the sarcasm in her voice.

Jo looked back down at her notebook.

Meg shot her mother a look. "Gonna take a quick shower before I eat my dinner."

I felt the awkwardness in the air and was relieved when I heard Grauntie say, "Well I think we'll be on our way. Oh, one more thing. Can you suggest a good ice cream place?"

"How about Bedford Farms Mom?" Beth said.

"Since you suggested it, that's where we'll head for breakfast!" Grauntie said. "It's a tradition for us. First morning in a new place we have ice cream."

I looked back at the yellow house as we walked away. Jo was still sitting on the porch swing writing. Beth was chasing Amy through the leaves. Meg had turned on lights upstairs.

"Why did Mrs. Conner seem so mad?" Charlie asked.

Grauntie shrugged her shoulders as she put her arm around Charlie. "Not sure. Maybe she just had a bad day."

6

EVENING IN CONCORD

Mandy went back inside to finish cleaning up after dinner and fix a plate of food for Nate to eat later. Seemed like he never got caught up, with work or with paying bills.

Jo sat down on the porch swing, pulling a throw over her lap to warm her as the evening air chilled. She was in the middle of working on a story about Julia Peabody.

Beth was playing with Amy. She was excited thinking about biking to the park tomorrow.

Meg was taking a nice long hot shower. She loved her work at the Maple Ridge Retirement Village. It was just a part-time job now, but maybe she'd go into a career working with older people. She laughed thinking about how funny they could be. Flo and Betty had her in stitches again today.

* * *

Nate Conner was still working on the house he was rehabbing just three blocks away. This late night work was getting exhausting. And he was missing too many dinners with the kids and Mandy.

He kicked himself when he saw he was running out of the stain he needed to finish the doors tonight. Should he call it a day or run over to his workshop and pick up more?

Taking a deep breath, and bending his shoulders back to stretch, Nate decided he might as well put in another hour. That would mean overnight drying time for the doors and he could hang them in the morning.

He climbed in his old pickup truck and drove over to the workshop.

He dreaded seeing Mandy's face when he walked in so late again tonight. Maybe she'd be asleep. He could tell how upset she was earlier when he had dropped Meg back at home and then left right away again.

Maybe having the Pameroy's in town would make her happy. She enjoyed showing off Concord to visitors.

At the Maple Ridge Retirement Village, all the residents

were in their little cottages. Flickering lights from televisions shown through windows. Dim lighting, directed downward, lit the walkways and upward lighting shown into the tall maples. All was quiet, the day winding down for the residents.

At least the day was ending for the majority of the elderly living at Maple Ridge. As with most things, there are exceptions. And Betty and Flo would be happy to hear they are considered the exception.

They had eaten the cheese, cracker and grape appetizer. They were still enjoying their second glasses of wine. The bottle was empty, so they sipped slower to relish the last of it. Wrapped in blankets, they sat outside of Flo's cottage soaking up the crisp fall evening air.

Their friendship and these late night visits had come about after Flo arrived a few months ago. Talk of making a break from here and getting a little house together had been hashed over, but both agreed this place wasn't so bad. The meals offered in the on-site restaurant were a convenience. They had their own one bedroom cottages instead of apartments or single rooms like a lot of retirement places had. Things were okay.

They agreed that getting away to a warmer climate during the cold winter months would be wonderful. But oh well, that might not happen, so they made the best of what they had here.

* * *

A cold wind was blowing in from the north, bringing a wintery feeling to those late diners and shoppers still walking about on Main Street. They walked faster and turtled into their coats, pulling the collars up around their necks.

A loose sheet of paper announcing the upcoming Halloween celebration skipped down the sidewalk, occasionally catching on straw bales then frantically fluttering until it shook itself free to continue on.

With deft swiftness a black leather shoe stomped down on it. The paper fought to get free before it was picked up by a gloved hand and held at reading height.

The man noted the Halloween celebration announcement. Lillia Pameroy had arrived at a perfect time he thought. All Hallow's Eve was always good for ghostly things. He crumbled the announcement, tossing it into a decorative trash can outside the Main Street Antique Store.

He was happy that Margaret had attracted Lillia's attention in the mirror. And he was pleased with his subsequent purchase of the initialed silver hand mirror just a few hours later.

Things were progressing nicely.

I stepped outside to our deck after Grauntie and Charlie went to bed. Wrapping myself in a blanket I plopped down on the large wooden Adirondack chair. Leaves skittered along on the driveway below me. Lingering bonfire smells drifted past.

I needed to get a feel for this place. After all, I was here to figure out if there were enough ghost stories and paranormal activity to support a ghost tour. So far there was the face in the mirror and the cradle thing.

Relax Lillia. You can focus better tomorrow. Charlie's off with Beth so you won't be tripping over him. Grauntie has some historical things she wants to see. For sure I want to get to the Sleepy Hollow Cemetery. Graves and cemeteries are always good for a ghost or two.

I was stepping back into our apartment when I

noticed headlights of a vehicle pulling up in front of the Peabody house. It stopped and the lights shut off. A door slammed.

When I realized someone was walking on the side of the house, I quickly stepped in and quietly closed our door. Using the dim light from Grauntie's digital photo frame I made my way to the window above the sink to peek out.

What should I do?

Who would come here at this hour?

The person moved toward our carriage house.

Should I wake Grauntie?

I breathed a sigh of relief when light spilled out an opened door below me. Must be Jo's dad Nate going into his workshop.

I had to laugh at myself. Too much ghost hunting on your mind!

8

FIRST MORNING ICE CREAM

The Bedford Farms Ice Cream Shop on Thoreau Street offered coffee as well as ice cream. The place was busy with locals getting their morning caffeine fix when Nora, Lillia and Charlie arrived. Young mothers with babies in strollers sat at the tables trying to catch a few minutes of adult conversation. Working people popped in, grabbing coffee to go.

Charlie picked out the Green Monster ice cream in honor of Halloween and Lillia choose Peanut Butter Cup.

Nora was still deciding on her flavor when she said, "Who came up with this idea of ice cream for breakfast instead of say eggs or French toast?"

Lillia and Charlie enjoyed a conspiring glance and made her wait longer.

"Hmm," Lillia finally said. "That might have been my

idea. Gosh when did this start? Do you remember Charlie?"

"I think it was on your first trip. That ice cream shop in Kentucky, right? I wasn't there but seems you told me about Peter Pottle."

"That's right! Now I remember. Peter was such a sweet guy." Lillia scooped another bite up from her bowl. Her spoon paused on the way up to her mouth. She looked at Grauntie Nora and started laughing. "You should see your face!"

"What?" Nora said, feigning disinterest.

"Of course, it was you who thought of it," Lillia said.

"And we love you for it," Charlie added. "I think it'll be a tradition on every trip I take forever and ever."

Mandy decided to pop in to Bedford Farm and make sure the Pameroy's were set for the day. She ordered a coffee to go at the busy counter before joining Nora at her table.

"Beth is counting on Charlie to take a bike ride with her. Might I suggest the Concord Museum for you Nora. It's a wonderful overview of our history."

Nora said, "The museum sounds like a perfect first stop. And it would be good for the kids to see too."

"But I'm supposed to go with Beth," Charlie pleaded. "I could always catch the museum later." Charlie kept his fingers crossed under the table top.

"Well, let me think. I'd like you to at least see some of it. Let's say half an hour with me at the museum then off you go."

Lillia said, "Plus then Grauntie, you can read all the signs in all the displays. Word by word. And look at every single solitary item in there without us hovering around and bothering you."

"Whoa, you paint quite a picture. Am I that bad? And does this mean you're abandoning me too?"

Mandy chuckled and shook her head. "You sound like my type of touring buddy. We'll get to the Orchard House on my day off. And I'll stay with you the whole time. Promise! Well gotta run now. Have a great day everyone!"

At the Concord Museum Charlie was most interested in the Revolutionary War area of the galleries.

One curator overheard Charlie asking if a half hour was up yet. He tapped Charlie on his shoulder and said, "Excuse me young man, but before you leave, perhaps you'd like to see a unique piece from the time of the war."

Lillia and Grauntie Nora followed behind as the curator led Charlie to another room. He was talking about Paul Revere's midnight ride and Charlie was telling him he had been studying that in school and would visit the North Bridge later today.

"Well young man, then this is the perfect thing for

you to see. Here we are." He stopped in front of an old corroded metal object.

"That looks like the lights hanging outside my garage at home. What's the big deal about it?" Charlie asked.

"Do you see it's holding a candle? And you've heard *the one if by land, two if by sea* thing?"

"Sure, that was a signal for which way the British would attack. Paul Revere needed to know so he could warn the others."

"Great Charlie. Since you know your history, you will appreciate the fact that this was one of the original signaling lanterns hanging in Boston's Old North Church."

Charlie eyes widened and his mouth dropped open. "Really? So, this was in the steeple in 1775?"

"Yes," the curator said. "Impressive piece of history isn't it?"

"I'll say," Charlie murmured.

9

LILLIA

Seeing the lantern impressed me too. But when Grauntie said Charlie could head out I let her know I wanted to leave and explore Sleepy Hollow Cemetery. "Okay, but can you walk Charlie over to the Conner's first?"

"Sure. I'm heading that way anyway to look for the path to the cemetery behind the Peabody house." I steered Charlie out the front door of the museum and he eagerly followed me to Mill Street.

Beth was sitting on the porch swing waiting and came running down the steps when she saw us. Amy bounded right behind her. Leaning against a tall red leaved maple were two bikes.

"Hey guys! Did you like the museum? I've been there a bunch of times. Schools around here use it a lot for field trips."

Charlie said, "I saw the signal lantern used to let Paul Revere know which way the British were going. That was cool."

I corrected him. "That was *one* of the lanterns that signaled to Paul Revere. Remember there were two?"

"Mere details," Beth said. "Right Charlie?"

Charlie gave her a thumbs up. "Mere details big sister! Ready to go?"

Beth pulled her bike up and in the same movement swung one leg over to reach the opposite pedal.

"See you later Lillia," Charlie called out as he climbed on the other bike and they pedaled away.

"Hold on guys!" I yelled. "Beth, the path behind the Peabody house leads to Sleepy Hollow, right?"

"It does. You have to walk through a swampy area and then you come out on the back end of it. Come on Charlie, I've got lots I want to show you."

I found the entry to the path. It appeared to be almost grown over, but after about twenty steps, it joined with a more heavily used path.

Soon I discovered wooden walkways and even little bridges. Reeds as tall as me and wispy grasses rose alongside the trail. The grasses were a soft golden color. At their roots fresh green sprouts appeared, not ready to declare the end of the growing season just yet.

I felt warm here, protected from the wind and catching the sunshine amongst the tall reeds.

Croaks and tiny little splashes let me know I wasn't alone. I hoped the cooler temperatures chased away any snakes that might linger here. Frogs okay. Snakes not so much!

I couldn't see above the reeds for most of the path, but when I looked back, I saw the Peabody house watching my progress from her perch atop the hill.

Beth had told me I couldn't miss the cemetery, just keep an eye out for a path to my left. I was thinking I'd had walked by it. How much further should I go?

Then there was it was, a little direction sign stuck in the earth with an arrow pointing left above the words *HISTORIC SLEEPY HOLLOW CEMETERY*. It wasn't long before the path climbed uphill. I left the swamp grasses behind and was soon among big trees.

On the grounds above me gray headstones stood. Some upright, other leaning. Narrow pathways wove around trees and past grave markers. When I got to the high point, I could see across the burial grounds to a highway far below.

After meandering for a bit, I noticed a marker telling me I was on Author's Ridge. Here were the graves of Hawthorne and Emerson. There was Louisa May Alcott's headstone and Henry David Thoreau's grave. Pencils and pens were resting near the markers. I bet those were left out of respect. Visitors who read the works of these famous authors wanted to leave a token behind.

These authors must have all known each other because Thoreau died in 1862 and Hawthorne in 1864. Alcott and Emerson died within six years of each other.

I'm sure Tiffany knows about these famous people though. She probably wants other ideas for a ghost tour. Hmm…maybe not? I'll have to ask her.

10

AT SLEEPY HOLLOW

Sitting with her back against the headstone, Jo stretched her arms high reaching for the tree branches overhead. Then she leaned forward, bending to reach across the journal lying on her lap. She touched her toes. Stretching felt good after she'd been sitting so long. The ground was cold under her.

But the whispers from Julia Peabody kept coming. She couldn't just walk away.

So, she shifted around, tucking her jacket further between her butt and the ground.

There that's better. Now what were you saying Julia? She listened.

Then she wrote. Adding more to the story she had been working on the past few days...

• • •

Anna and Louisa May Alcott took me to spend the day with Mr. Thoreau at his beloved Walden Pond. He shared with us the most delightful things about nature. Why I never even knew more than three types of mushrooms. Now I know so very many more. He is kind and patient. The pond is pleasant, and we all intend to go rowing together once summer has arrived.

Mr. Thoreau encouraged us to live richly, yet simply, in nature. His cabin in the woods near Walden Pond is certainly a testament to his desire to observe and learn about nature by living amongst the flora and fauna of the forests in a self-sustaining manner.

On our walk back to Concord, Louisa May shared news she had received from a neighbor boy. She learned that George Peabody's aunt, who recently married, had left to live with her new husband in parts of our country far to the West. Louisa May breathlessly expressed her feelings that she would embrace such an adventure whole heartedly. Anna and I however, agreed it would not be for us. I love being home in Concord and do not have the same wanderlust Louisa May possesses.

After much giggling and chatter amongst the three of us, I confessed to them that I found George Peabody to be a most engaging companion. The Alcott sisters immediately assured me that they would more frequently invite George to join us on our Walden Ponds excursions. They are the dearest friends!

Mother has noticed that I am interested in George and suggested that we...

Jo slammed her journal shut and stood. Walking on the ridge above her was the visitor from Kansas, Lillia Pameroy. *Why is she here by herself?*

Lillia waved when she saw Jo and walked down toward her.

"Hi Jo. Do you come here often to write?" Lillia asked.

"It's peaceful here." She dropped her pencil and bent to retrieve it when she heard Julia whisper, *visit tomorrow and I'll tell you more.*

Lillia looked around. "What was that sound?"

Was Lillia able to hear the whispering here too? Maybe she wasn't alone in what she heard.

But Lillia quickly dismissed whatever it was she thought she heard. "Hmm, maybe just rustling leaves. I was exploring Author's Ridge. Kind of neat how those authors all lived here."

"My father is named after one buried there. Can you guess which one?" Jo said.

"Has to be Nathaniel Hawthorne. Right?" Lillia said. "Your dad was working late last night. I heard him in his workshop underneath us."

"Yeah, he's works late a lot of nights."

"What does he do?" Lillia asked.

"He does remodeling jobs. Loves restoration work, fixing up old places. But those sorts of jobs dried up. Now he does the basic stuff, like finish off basements. Or add a bathroom."

"Why doesn't he work on that big old abandoned house by us?" Lillia asked.

"He was supposed to. He bought it cheap. But then with the recession things changed. Now Mom calls it a money pit." Jo shifted away from the painful subject of the Peabody house. "I heard yesterday you were here to find ghosts. That's cool."

Lillia said, "Do you know of any good Concord ghost stories? Or write any?"

Jo hesitated. How she heard her stories could be considered a ghostly thing. She preferred to think of the grave whisperings as her muse, her inspiration. But she was beginning to suspect it was more than that.

Lillia waited for an answer, before saying, "Sorry. I didn't mean to put you on the spot. Maybe you don't believe in paranormal stuff. But sitting here in a cemetery to write, I figured it might interest you."

Jo held back on telling Lillia about the whispers she heard from the dead people. It sounded so weird if she said it out loud. "It's quiet here. Peaceful. Fewer distractions than home. And I feel like the people buried here all have their stories."

"Interesting way to look at it. You're right. Everyone has a story," Lillia said.

Jo panned her hands across the cemetery. "There are hundreds of graves so hundreds of stories. It feels inspiring for me."

"What are you working on now?" Lillia asked as she looked around at the nearby headstones.

Jo stepped over and pointed at a low-lying headstone. "I'm writing a story about her, Julia Peabody."

11

LILLIA

I read the headstone. *"Julia Peabody.* Do you think she lived in the abandoned house your dad bought?"

Reaching for her jacket lying on the ground, Jo said, "I'm not sure. But as for my fictitious Julia, I'll see where the story takes me."

"That's neat. I wish I could write stories."

"What is cool is being a ghost hunter like you. Why would Tiffany ask you to check Concord out for ghosts?"

"We met in San Antonio where she runs a terrific ghost tour and she's been looking to expand her business."

"But I mean why wouldn't she check out Concord on her own?"

Oh boy, how do I answer that question? The reason involves my special imagining abilities which I rarely share. It's usually not ended well when I did. Kids would laugh at me, or worse, think I was crazy. And then Mom's reaction of fear was something that never left her. It still hangs between us.

Jo could see I was reacting oddly. She said, "I'm not prying, just curious."

"It's not you. It's just that I don't know how to explain what all happened in Texas."

"I'd love to hear if you find any ghosts here. I guess this cemetery would be a good place to do it. Well I've got to be heading home. I'm glad we got to see each other again."

"Can I join you on your walk out? I'll explain a little more about what happened in Texas if you'd like to hear."

"Sure," Jo said. "I'd love that."

I had a good feeling about Jo. She was creative, made up stories. And even sat in graveyards to write!

"My Grauntie and I were invited to San Antonio, Texas to help a friend's cousin whose uncle was a night guard at the Alamo. While we were there Grauntie and I did the tourist stuff. Including ghost tours. San Antonio is one of the most haunted cities in the United States."

Jo said, "Excuse me, but why do you call her Grauntie?

I laughed. "Well it is a mix up of great-aunt and grandaunt. You know like Grandmother turns into

Grandma and Grammie? I mushed them together and came up with Grauntie!"

Jo nodded. "Cute. She's important to you. I can tell."

"You've got that right."

"I'd love to go on a ghost tour sometime. We only have historical tours here," Jo said.

"Will they do one at the cemetery on Halloween night?" I asked.

"I don't know. I'd like to go if they do. Let me ask Mom when she gets home tonight. She knows everything that's going on in Concord."

"Let's make plans to go together," I suggested.

Jo smiled. "I'd like that. Sorry I interrupted you. Go on. What happened in San Antonio?"

"After we took Tiffany's tour, she thought I had a kind of radar for ghostly goings on." I shrugged to minimize the comment. "So, she asked me to check Concord out for her."

Jo stopped and looked directly at me. "I've got a feeling there's more to that story. What is this radar for ghostly goings on as you call it?"

At twelve-years-old I am learning to read people and how they will react. Is that what growing up means? Jo sure picked up on stuff I was trying to be evasive about. How much should I tell her?

"It's sort of odd sounding when I try to explain it."

"Kind of odd like me sitting in the cemetery to write?"

"Yeah, kind of like that." I fumbled to find the right words, but then I remembered the cold book story.

"Things seem to come to me, enter my radar. Like once I discovered fake books. This guy George Vanderbilt built a humongous home, the Biltmore. In his library he had thousands of books. One of them was Hawthorne's *The Scarlet Letter*. It felt cold. And that helped me figure out it was a fake."

"What's a cold book? What do you mean a fake book? A book is a book isn't it?" Jo said.

"Right, but antique or new was the difference. Long story short, a man there was sneaking out valuable books to sell on the black market and he made up fake ones so he wouldn't be discovered. *The Scarlet Letter* book felt different, cooler to my touch. My learning that helped solve a cold case for a detective."

"Wow! That's so neat. You helped a detective!"

Jo didn't grasp what I tried hinting at, my special abilities. Choosing my next words carefully I said, "Yes, but I was really in San Antonio to find out what spirits were trying to reach Pedro at the Alamo."

The words hung in the air between us. What was she thinking?

"You communicate with spirits?" Jo said in a soft, reverend voice.

I nodded. She hadn't laughed at me. Good. "In a way. But Jo, so often people tease me, or make me feel stupid about it. They call my imaginings my special ability but say it in a snarky way."

Jo looked nervous. "Not me. I'm not mean like that."

12

AFTERNOON IN CONCORD

Meanwhile, back across town, Charlie and Beth pedaled along on the bike path that wove through the Minute Man Historical Park.

"This bridge doesn't look very old," Charlie said when they arrived at the North Bridge.

"It's not. They put the last one up just before I was born."

That disappointed Charlie. "What other things here aren't real? I mean like Disney world makes things look old, but it's faked. I didn't get it that things here might not actually be old."

Beth said, "Oh my gosh, you didn't expect an old wooden bridge, that people used every day, to survive hundreds of years?"

"Well the houses here are old and are made of wood. They're still standing."

"Ah dah. No one walks over them every day."

"Yah, guess you're right," Charlie said.

Beth started pushing her bike across the bridge, but stopped to point out the famous poem about the shot heard round the world etched into the base of a tall monument.

"The guy who wrote this poem, Emerson, lived in Concord and is buried up in Sleepy Hollow," she said. "Come on Charlie, let's cross over, I want to show you the Minuteman Statue on the other side."

"So that's what the soldiers looked like. Not much of a uniform," Charlie said, gazing up at a life size statue.

"Don't you remember Charlie? I thought you just got done studying the American Revolution. These guys were more like volunteers than soldiers. The colonies didn't have a big army you know."

Charlie shrugged. "We learned that, but when you're sitting in a fourth-grade classroom in Kansas, all the details don't register."

"They were ready at a minute's notice to fight for their country's independence!" Beth exclaimed, throwing her arms up toward the statue. "Leaving their fields and farms to join the battle. Brave men ready to give…"

"What's that thing at his feet?" Charlie interrupted.

Beth exhaled and sighed before saying, "A plow Charlie. Aren't you inspired by this statue? And that bridge across the mighty Concord River? And the...oh I don't know, just all of it!"

"I am. Guess I'm maybe a little jealous. You get to live right in the middle of where it all went on."

Beth said, "I hadn't thought about that. I am lucky that way." She grinned and gave Charlie a fist bump. "Glad I can show this to you. But now we should start back to town."

But Beth made one more stop to point out a marker. "Charlie, this is something you might want to see. It's a monument stone for the British soldiers that died and were buried here."

Charlie read the words etched on the stone...

> *They came three thousand miles and died,*
> *To keep the past upon its throne.*
> *Unheard beyond the ocean tide,*
> *Their English mother made her moan.*

"That's sad," Charlie said, looking up at Beth. "How strange it must be. Buried so far away from your home. All alone here. Left behind."

The two left and rode away toward Main Street.

After a few minutes Beth asked, "Want to go trick-or-treating with me?"

"Sure, I'll go. But I don't have a costume."

"Last year I was a scarecrow. But like a vampire one. It was great. We should be able to round up old clothes for you."

Charlie said. "Hey, I could go as a Minuteman! Old clothes would do that. And maybe a toy rifle."

"Or the plow," Beth said with a laugh.

"No way!"

They carefully skirted around others on the path walking dogs or pushing strollers.

The bike path turned and took the two young riders pass the Maple Ridge Retirement Village where old people sitting in rockers waved at them.

A man in a dark suit tipped his small round hat at them.

* * *

Mandy was finishing paperwork at the antique store. Well this is good news she thought as she went through receipts. That engraved silver hand mirror sold, and we got a good price for it. I knew it was a valuable piece when I came across it at the Peabody house. Thank goodness that old dump pulled in a couple of bucks. Not even close to covering the upkeep and restoration on the house though.

Wonder who bought that mirror? Mandy walked to the back where Helen was working. "Helen, did you handle the sale of that silver mirror yesterday?"

"The one with the P initial engraved on it? Yes, I did. And for full price. No quibbling at all."

"Good job. Who bought it?"

"Kind of odd fellow. Very proper in his speech and behavior. Wearing an old-fashioned black suit with one of those funny little round hats. He carried a walking stick and had the cutest British accent. He was super happy to find it, in that restrained British way."

"Oh really? Glad you got it sold."

"He even asked me for a magnifying glass and carefully went over Paul Revere's mark and all the engraved details. Took a long time with it. I sensed it had a personal connection for him."

"Bowler," Mandy said.

Helen squinted her eyes and gave Mandy a puzzled look.

"That's what they call the hat. A bowler. They were common in England years ago."

"Oh!" Helen laughed. "Yep that sounds right. Oh, and he asked all sorts of questions. Where we got the mirror from? Was it part of a set? Did we have any more pieces?"

Helen leaned across the paper filled desktop. "In fact, he asked me to give this to anyone who might be interested. If I would be so kind he says. Isn't that just the cutest way to say please?"

She handed a sheet of paper to Mandy.

Nate went to the front door of the Peabody house. His money pit as Mandy called it. It sat empty for decades before it came up in a tax sale. When the Peabody house was put on the auction block, it was a once in a lifetime thing. Nate bought it. Now he had to face the hard cold facts. His dream of restoring the old gal wasn't meant to be.

He glanced over his shoulder at the carriage house. At least he had the space there for his work shop. If things didn't get better at home, he'd use the little apartment as a getaway from Mandy's nagging.

His passion was for restoring buildings, bringing them back to life. When he started his own restoration business things went well. Until they didn't. It was like the economy hit a wall and collapsed

He wasn't alone during those times. Money tightened

up for everyone. He started basic remodeling to keep food on the family's table. Luckily Mandy inherited her mom's antique shop and that brought in a little more income.

Nate unlocked the door and switched on his flashlight. His dreams of restoring this beauty and opening a bed and breakfast were fading fast. He was sad about that, but the taxes alone were putting a big dent in their finances.

He came here more often lately...to begin the letting go process.

13

LILLIA

"I'm glad you told me. Shared your story," Jo said.

I said, "So am I."

Jo didn't say anything more, but put her journal in her backpack.

We started walking along the path that ran to back of the cemetery and were on the swamp trail when Jo spoke next. "You talked about your imaginings. I'm guessing they are paranormal things?" Jo stopped to look at me.

I nodded.

"Lillia, I come to the cemetery for more than the peace and quiet. Something else happens there."

She seemed hesitant to tell me more, but I finally asked, "What happens?"

"The stories come when I'm still and waiting. When I listen."

"Isn't that how authors write? They are inspired in their brain and think the story? So, you're listening to your brain."

"I used to think of it like that. But it's more than inspiration Lillia. And it's not all in my head."

I felt goosebumps rising on my arms. "Tell me what it is Jo."

"I hear whispers from them...the buried people." Jo looked down at the ground and started walking again.

I walked along with her, praying she would feel okay to tell me more.

"I came to Sleepy Hollow to read names and dates on the headstones. To try imaging what went on in the person's life. If a couple died on the same date, were they in an accident together? Or a wife who died years before her husband. Was he lonely? Did he wilt away? I made up stories from my thoughts."

"That's not so strange. What changed?"

In a low voice, that I had to strain to hear, Jo said, "The whispers started a few months ago. I didn't recognize it at first. Like I'd think the sound was traffic coming up the hill. Or trees rustling in the wind."

I nodded, giving her assurance to continue.

"Once I let myself really listen for the whispers, I heard their stories."

"And now today, Julia Peabody was whispering to you?"

"Yes. Do you believe me? I mean about hearing them?"

"I believe you Jo. I believe they are whispering to you. We both communicate with spirits but in different ways."

I could hear her sigh of relief.

"Tell me how you communicate Lillia."

And as we walked, I told her about my imaginings coming from the energies people leave behind. I told more about the spirits at the Alamo and others.

When we came out on to the back lawn of the Peabody house, she pulled papers out of her backpack and handed them to me.

"This is some of the story from that first whisperer… it's not finished, but I'd like you to read it and let me know what you think."

I took the papers.

"And Lillia, you can tell me the truth," Jo said. "See you tomorrow?"

"Yep. I'll read this tonight," I said.

And later that evening I read…

The Peabody's of Concord
By Josephine Conner

No one lived in the house on Mill Street after Norma Peabody passed away. They buried her body in Sleepy Hollow Cemetery on a cold and rainy New England day. The winds strong enough to cause men to grab their hats and ladies to require help handling their umbrellas.

Some believe grief on the day of a funeral can be less oppressive for those in attendance if the sun is shining. There are inherent feelings of joyfulness under a clear blue sky. Funeral attendees might struggle to feel serious or somber.

The weather on the day of Norma's burial encouraged the handful of black-clothed mourners to behave with a proper note of grim sadness. Irregardless whether the feelings were induced by mourning or by dreary weather, Norma would have been satisfied with the ceremony.

Though few knew where that image of Norma Peabody as a lonely bitter spinster started, no one concerned themselves enough to visit her. She had been dead for five days before her body was discovered.

The story that follows is part of an oral history shared within the Peabody family.

I chose to put it in writing as best I could as it would seem that Norma is the last of the Concord Peabody's.

In 1775 Margaret and Cornelius Peabody, Norma's great-great-grandparents, were married in Lancaster,

England. For newly married couples coming from a comfortable level of wealth, the customary honeymoon was an extended tour to a foreign land. Mr. and Mrs. Peabody sailed across the Atlantic Ocean to the British colony of Massachusetts to visit with family friends.

They heard of unrest in the colonies from Margaret's father who owned several merchant ships that plied the Atlantic. Word of colonists' and rebels' aggressive acts in Boston Harbor during the Boston Tea Party did not deter Margaret and Cornelius. They set sail from St. George's Quay on the River Lune on a blustery spring morning.

Margaret attributed her queasy feelings en route to seasickness and was relieved to arrive in Boston and see the lovely cherry trees in blossom.

Upon arrival in Boston, Margaret's husband surprised her with a special gift. He had commissioned a silver vanity set from the local and renowned silversmith Paul Revere. The pieces were beautifully designed and crafted. Exquisite engraved detailing included the initial P in the bright polished silver surface of the mirror, brush, comb and nail file. Margaret knew she would treasure it forever.

The young couple settled in and began a social whirl meeting prominent British Bostonians. They attended church services at the Old North Church and spent pleasant afternoons strolling in Boston Commons.

Those in the young couple's circle continued to hear whis-

pers of trouble stirring within the colonial population. When Cornelius was ordered to join the British troops gathering in the harbor, he felt his national pride swell and immediately kissed his young bride goodbye. He marched to the harbor with his head held high. Margaret's heart soared with pride and ached with fear.

When traitors to the British crown were discovered to be meeting in the Lexington area, the Queen's troops marched inland. Cornelius was one of them. He left not knowing his young wife was pregnant with their son.

A week passed before Margaret learned that her husband Cornelius died in a skirmish in a little village called Concord. Her heart was broken into a thousand pieces. Her father back in England begged her to return on the next ship sailing out of Boston Harbor.

She hesitated, knowing she needed to see the burial site of her husband and the other British soldiers who had perished in battle. When it was deemed safe, she hired a carriage and rode the very road the troops had marched on. She passed through the charming little village of Concord.

Her dear husband's spirit had left the earth here and here she would stay to make a life for herself. Soon Margaret learned that a new independent country was being formed, she decided to stay and become an American citizen. She could not leave Cornelius behind.

14

THE PEABODY HOUSE

Beth and Charlie were looking for Nate to ask him about going into the old house to hunt for Halloween costumes. He wasn't home but Mandy suggested they check at his workshop in the carriage house.

Beth was first to notice a light in the front window of the Peabody house. "Dad must be in there doing his restoration dreaming. Mom says he dreams too much and restores too little."

Charlie said, "How come he doesn't work on it? If you love doing something so much don't you just do it?"

Beth looked up at the house. "I know money is tight for us right now, so he's always working at jobs that pay him. Is your family rich Charlie? Sounds like you and Lillia travel around a lot."

Charlie nodded. "Yeah, we do. But not as a family. It's

always with Grauntie. She's family, but I mean without Mom and Dad. I guess we're okay. Dad works a lot. He's goes to conventions and conferences and all that. He takes me fishing sometimes, but usually he likes to get away with his buddies."

Beth dropped her bike on the carpet of leaves covering the house's front lawn. "Come on, let's go in and find Dad." She ran up to the open front door. "Dad? You in here?"

"Hey Beth. Come on in."

Old rugs were rolled up and piled against the wall. Several boxes sat next to them. Nate rested on the first step of the stairs that led to the darkness of the second floor.

"Hey guys. Did you have fun today?" Nate said.

"We did. I took Charlie through town and into the park. We saw the North Bridge and that Minuteman Statue. That's what Charlie wants to be for Halloween."

"A bridge?" Nate asked.

Beth rolled her eyes. "No Dad, a minuteman. I remember mom saying there were lots of old clothes left here. I told Charlie maybe we could find something for him to wear."

Charlie, taking in the old abandoned feeling of the house said, "This would make a great haunted house Mr. Conner. You could hang skeletons and spider webs and sell tickets. The yard is so big you could have a maze here. My sister and I love the fall corn mazes we go through back in Kansas."

"That's a great idea. We could charge admission and you'd make some money to restore it Dad," Beth added.

Nate laughed, at least Beth was still cheering for him to keep the house. "Thanks, but I think I'll pass on that idea."

"Is the house haunted?" Charlie asked. "My sister is looking for ghosts."

Nate said, "I don't know if it's haunted, but I know a little bit about the woman who died here."

He took his flashlight and put the beam under his chin, throwing up scary shadows. "Hmm, maybe she'll want to meet your sister. I'll ask her."

He spun the light beam up the stairs and circled it in crazy spinning shapes. "Nooorrrmmmmaaa...are you here?"

Beth screamed.

Charlie jumped back.

"Dad, stop that!" Beth punched her dad in the shoulder.

"Someone died here? In this house?" Charlie swallowed, his eyes wide and scanning the room.

Beth was excited. "I bet it's haunted then. If she died right in this house. Tell us the story Dad."

"Her name was Norma Peabody. I found paperwork in an upstairs room that told me Margaret Peabody built the house right after the American Revolution. I found other old correspondence too. Margaret and her husband Cornelius were originally from Britain. He died here. I found letters from their families back in England asking her to return home. It appears she stayed put here in Concord."

Beth said. "How come you bought her house Dad? Didn't her family want it?"

"She didn't have a will, and no family came forward after she passed away. It looked like she just lived her last days here all alone. Sort of sad."

Charlie asked, "What are you going to do with this place?"

Nate put down the flashlight. "Sell it."

Then he looked at Charlie and Beth with a smile. "You two can rummage through any old clothes and make yourselves some Halloween costumes. But it'll have to wait until daylight. There's no electricity to the house."

Beth and her dad headed home as Charlie walked to the apartment above the carriage house.

Lillia was sitting on the couch reading.

Charlie started telling her about the old lady who had died in the Peabody house, but Grauntie stopped him.

"Save that for later," Grauntie said. "Dinner is ready. I

made traditional Boston baked beans. Got some yummy clam chowder, along with a lobster roll from Twin Seafood in town."

Charlie started to protest, but again Grauntie stopped him. "Not to worry! For my less adventuresome young ones' taste buds, I heated up hot dogs. But I want you both to try the seafood. You should always try local foods when you travel. You might enjoy it. End of my sermon. Now eat!"

Because of the fresh air on his bike ride, Charlie fell asleep early without telling Lillia and Grauntie about the haunted house.

15

LILLIA

I was glad when morning came. I hardly slept last night because I kept thinking about the terrific story Jo wrote. The words really sounded like an adult talking to her. But Jo never talked to a living Norma Peabody! Clever how she used the term oral family history, instead of saying whispers from a grave.

She described the exact mirror I saw in the antique store. The mirror that showed me the morphing woman. That person I saw could have been Margaret Peabody.

After breakfast, Grauntie said, "I'm going to meet Mandy at the antique store and if she can get away, she's taking me out to Walden Pond. I'm excited. I read Thoreau's books when I was in high school and found a great deal of inspiration from them. Do you two want to go with us? Maybe the forest around the pond is full of ghosts!"

I said, "I'm headed over to Jo's now. I'll touch base with you and see if she wants to go."

"No thanks, Grauntie, Beth and I are putting our Halloween costumes together today, so we'll be busy," Charlie said.

Jo was happy to hear I liked the story. "How much more do you know about the house and the family?" I asked her.

"Well I know Norma was the last Peabody to live there. I listened to her and then, this was so strange, but one day I couldn't hear her anymore...at her grave I mean."

"That's too bad. You may never know the rest of the story about how she ended up like that, all alone."

"You know the Julia Peabody grave I was by when you saw me yesterday? I think she's Norma's mother."

"Really? What is Julia telling you?"

Jo said, "Her story is jumbled. I can show it to you later if you want. It's hard to tell where Julia's voice starts and my storytelling takes over. It blurs. Sometimes I think Norma got mad at me and stopped whispering because I was writing her story wrong. She didn't seem like a very pleasant or patient person."

"Jo, don't doubt what you hear. In fact, I have something to prove you are not just making up stuff." I grabbed her by the hand. "Come with me to your Mom's store. You'll like what I have to show you."

As we walked toward Main Street, I explained what I'd experienced when I was in the store that first day. How the cabinet holding the mirror seemed to rattle. And then when I held the mirror, what I saw in it. A woman morphing from a young bride into an elderly person with gray hair and wrinkles.

"Because I read the description in your story, I think that might have been Margaret."

Jo had a hopeful look on her face. "I can't wait to see the mirror. That's pretty crazy. But you're right. It would help me stop doubting myself. Maybe I should start a family tree and try to figure out how they all fit together."

"Can we get in the Peabody house and look around later? I love old places like that and maybe we'd find out clues to help fill in your stories."

Jo said, "Sure, I know where Dad keeps a spare key."

Mandy greeted us as soon as we stepped inside. "So, what are you two up to?"

"Hi Mom. Lillia wanted to show me something she saw here," Jo said as we headed back to the glass-fronted cabinet.

The mirror was gone!

I raced back to Mandy and described the mirror I'd held that first day.

"I'll be darn. Helen sold it that same day! Isn't that something? After months of it hanging around suddenly it's attracting all this attention."

I was so disappointed to hear it was gone. I wanted Jo to see it. It was spooky how much it was like the one she described in her story.

"Why did you want to see it again?" Mandy asked.

"I read one of Jo's stories and she described a piece just like it in there."

Jo quickly said, "Just a coincidence, I guess. No big deal."

By the way she was acting I knew she didn't want her mother asking too many questions.

Mandy said, "Doesn't she write great stories? I'm so happy she's sharing them with you. She usually keeps them to herself."

"That's Mom for you," Jo said, looking embarrassed. I decided I'd let it drop.

Mandy asked if we wanted to go site seeing with her and Grauntie, but Jo told her that she planned on taking me inside the Peabody house.

"Did you know that's where I found the silver mirror?" Mandy said.

"Are you serious? From Dad's house? I mean the

Peabody house? I had no idea," Jo said with a gasp.

My mouth fell open. I couldn't believe it either. "Really?"

The little bell above the door jingled and Mandy turned to greet the customers coming in as Jo and I moved past her.

"What did I tell you? Too many things fit to be just a coincidence," I said when we got out to the sidewalk.

Jo stood there wide-eyed. "I'll admit this is pretty weird. Maybe this would be a good ghost story line for Tiffany to hear about."

"The cemetery! We forgot to ask your mom about a Halloween tour there," I said. "Let's go back. Halloween is tomorrow and I want to sign up if they have one."

But when we turned to go back, I saw Helen come running toward us waving a piece of paper. "I overheard your conversation with your mom. Here, this is a copy of some information left by the customer who bought the mirror. Kind of an interesting story. Maybe you two can make something of it? Keep it. I made copies."

Jo and I sat on the nearest bench to look over the flyer. It was in black and white. The paper was yellowed and had an unusually soft feel to it. At the top was a letterhead with the name of a law firm and with an address in Lancaster, England.

Below that, in bold letters...

REWARD OFFERED FOR FAMILY HEIRLOOM

Next was a hand-drawn sketch of a vanity set comprising a mirror, a brush, a comb and a nail file. It included a detailed drawing of the intricacy of the silver-work, including the letter P in the design's center.

The writing below the sketch was faded and hard to read. But we did our best.

We figured out that the set was crafted in 1775 by Paul Revere. There were some other words that were too faint to read. But we found a section that said whoever possessed the pieces of the set should contact the firm in England immediately.

"This is weird," Jo said. "It's such unusual looking typing and odd wording. I'm not sure what we're reading."

We couldn't make out any further information until a hand-written note at the bottom requesting that those owning the pieces contact a Mr. Burgess at 289 Mill St. Concord MA, USA regarding these matters. A phone number had also been added at the bottom.

"Jo this is no longer coincidence. This is part of Margaret's story! She came from Lancaster. And had a vanity set like this."

A look of nervousness clouded Jo's face.

16

MAPLE RIDGE

Betty and Flo sat in comfy chairs on the porch of their retirement village welcome center. It was a favorite way to spend the afternoon as it afforded them the chance to keep their fingers on the pulse of Concord as Betty liked to say.

Flo saw Meg walking up and called out to her. "We saw your little sister bike by yesterday. Who was that handsome young man she was with?"

"Someone visiting us from Kansas. His sister is here looking for ghosts."

"Ghosts? How about us? We're almost ghosts! Right Betty Boo?"

Meg laughed. "Ah not even close! You two are the most full of life old people I know."

"That's a good thing," Flo said. "And our plans

include being full of life even after we are ghosts. Years from now, when we're long gone, you bet your booty you'll see these rockers tipping forward and back all afternoon."

"And if you see a random wine glass or two float by, it's just us toasting to your health!" Betty added.

"I bet you two will have some tricks up your sleeves," Meg said joining in the joke.

"Speaking of tricks, since Halloween is almost here, can we send you on an errand for us to pick up candy for the little ghosts and goblins?" Flo asked Meg.

"Sure thing. Let me write down what you want."

She reached in her purse for a piece of paper. "Oops, almost forgot. Mom gave me this copy of some information she wanted me to circulate here."

Meg handed the paper to Flo. "Now what kind of candy should I pick up for you two?"

Betty put in their order. Bag of Snickers. Bag of Reese's. Bag of bubble gum. "Flo, that sound like enough?"

Flo was still reading over the paper in her hand. "Sounds good. We'll reimburse you tomorrow. You're such a dear to help us out. Betty take a look at this," Flo said, handing the paper over to Betty. "Read that first line. Where did you say you got this Meg?"

"Mom gave it to me. A customer left it at the antique store."

"Did she say anything more about it?" Flo asked.

"Not really. Just that the guy bought a fancy hand mirror and is trying to complete some sort of vanity set. What is a vanity set anyway?"

"A vanity set was what people called grooming tools. It used to be quite the cat's meow to have fancy ones. Now combs and brushes are a dime a dozen. They were treasured luxuries back in the day."

Betty held up the paper for Meg to see. "Look at this sketch. That's a vanity set."

Meg took the piece of paper. Her forehead scrunched up. "What am I reading here? It's such a bad copy."

Flo took the paper back. "Best I can figure out is that someone is trying to find the whole set. Good luck with that. Says Revere made this in the 1700s. People move and things get lost. I can't imagine anyone ever finds the rest of it."

"Flo dear, I know just who might actually have seen a true luxurious vanity set in her life." Betty said.

"Abigail!" Flo and Betty said at the same time and gave each other a high five.

17

LILLIA

I said, "The mirror this man bought wasn't just any mirror. It's part of the Peabody story Jo. I just know it!"

Her expression shifted. She looked out over the street. Across the bales of straw and the decorated stalks of corn. Over the piles of pumpkins and fall mums. She seemed to be taking it all in with a new vision.

"Lillia, I'm feeling more and more like we are on to something. I wrote that story months ago. Maybe this was meant to be."

"What was meant to be?"

Jo turned toward me, confusion written all over her face. "Us. Something pulled you to that mirror in Mom's shop. And something spoke to me in the cemetery. I don't understand it, but it feels real. Does that make sense?"

I understood her confusion. I didn't know what was

going on either. Between seeing Margaret in the mirror and this information from the buyer, I knew there was a mystery to solve.

"The pieces that keep coming to you and to me, are trying to point us toward something. We each are bringing a special ability to this partnership Jo. I say let's keep working together and see if we can solve this mystery and find the missing vanity set pieces."

"Okay partner!" Jo said. "Mill Street is my street. And that house number would mean it's close to us. So let me think which way the numbers go…" She looked like she was struggling to say what thought was coming to her.

"Jo what is it?"

"I ah…it can't be right. I think that's the actual address of the Peabody house." Her hand flew to her mouth as she gasped.

"Jo, if that's true, this is taking a very strange turn. No one is living there," I said.

"But could there be something else waiting at that address?"

"We need to get in the house," I said. "I've got a strong feeling that whoever left this note on the paper wants us to go to the house. Maybe there will be more clues there. Clues about a vanity set!"

18

MEETING ABIGAIL

Back on the porch at Maple Ridge, Meg heard Flo and Betty say the name Abigail just as it came to her mind too. Abigail was a resident of Maple Ridge Retirement Village and if anyone here had a silver engraved vanity set in their past, it would be her.

"Speak of the devil," Flo said. "There she is now."

Coming across one of the brick paths from the cottages was a slightly stooped woman walking with careful steps. Her white hair pinned up in an elegant French twist above her pearl necklace. She wore a cardigan sweater set in an appropriate fall color over a wool plaid skirt.

Maple Ridge residents had often wondered why she was here and not on some fancy estate with maids and caregivers to help her. That seemed more the type of person her appearance projected. With the way she carried herself and dressed, it would seem she came from wealth.

If they had observed more closely, they might have noticed that her skirt was decades old in style. But it was a classic cut so that wasn't too obvious. The cardigan sleeve edges and elbow areas worn thin. Her leather pumps polished to cover the years of wear they had seen.

"She'd have her nose in the air if she wasn't so stooped over," Betty said.

It shocked Meg to hear her talk that way. "Betty, that's just plain mean.

Betty rolled her eyes. "From the mouth of babes. Sorry Meg, but there's just an uppityness about her. I've tried to talk with her or invite her to join us for a game of cards. She barely responds. Like it would be beneath her or something."

"Do you know she's very hard of hearing? And her eyesight is getting worse?" Meg said.

"Well tell her to get new hearing aids and glasses then. Get with it," Flo said.

"She might not have the money. Have you ever thought of that?" Meg said.

"Just look at her. Always with the pearl necklace and diamond stud earrings, dressed like she's going to a fancy lunch."

Meg didn't know how much to share with Flo and Betty. She knew Abigail dressed up every day because it was the way she felt best. It was what she was used to. Even if it was the same few pieces of clothing, a woman dressed a certain way...always. She was keeping up appearances.

Meg also knew Abigail needed, but couldn't afford, hearing aids and new glasses. The story as Meg understood it was that the family wealth had been lost in bad investments. Abigail wanted no sympathy, neither did she deserve to be treated like she was a snob. She craved company and friendship too. Her hearing loss made it such a struggle to communicate so more and more she stayed to herself.

"Well then Ms. Meg Conner, take her the paper and read it to her. Don't forget to shout in her ear," Betty said.

Meg thought I'll do one better. She walked over to where Abigail stood and with added volume in her voice said, "Excuse me, but would you mind joining Flo and Betty? I'm going over some information my mother asked me share with the residents here."

Abigail gently touched Meg's hand and said, "Maybe later dear. I'm just enjoying the sunset."

Meg kept trying. "There's an empty rocker next to them and you can see the sunset from there too. I think you might find the information interesting."

"If you say so. Are you sure they won't think I'm intruding?" Her eyes had a nervous fluttery quality. Meg took her by the arm. "Of course not Abigail. They hope to solve a mystery and thought you seemed like someone who understands the subject."

"Oh my, that sounds interesting. I love a good mystery. I read mystery books all the time. Big print now of course. And I love those British mystery TV channels."

Meg started walking with Abigail toward Flo and Betty. "So do they! See there, you have something in common already."

Abigail stood awkwardly in front of Betty and Flo as Meg arranged a rocking chair for her.

19

LILLIA

"Do you think your dad will mind us going in?" I asked Jo as we walked up the hill.

Jo thought a moment. "I don't think so. I'll just tell him we're looking for antiques to sell."

I was glad to be on our way to discovering more about the mysterious story of the vanity set. Who had the other three pieces? Why was someone across the ocean trying to put the set back together?

The workroom door was open, and Jo emerged holding the key high in her hand. "Got it."

We walked through the back door. It surprised me how the place felt like someone had just left it. So much stuff lying around the kitchen.

"So Jo, do you hear whispers in places like this?"

"Nope. But I feel the sense of what this house saw. The stories are in the walls, and the closets and the furniture," Jo said as she walked through the dim interior. "What about you? Are you getting any of those imaginings?"

I laughed. It was nice to have someone who knew about me. "Not yet!"

"The bedrooms are upstairs. I think Mom took anything of antique value out, but we could start by looking in the master bedroom I guess."

I could tell someone had been doing a few things in the house. Rolled up rugs, packing boxes and a few cleaning supplies stood in the hall. "What are your dad's plans for this place?"

"He's really into what he calls pragmatic restoration," Jo said.

"What's that mean?"

Jo said, "He wants to keep the feel and look of the original place, but with practical modern things added to it. He dreamed about making this into a place where people can stay. I think they're called bed and breakfast houses."

We climbed the creaky staircase to the second floor. This wasn't anything like the Biltmore Mansion, all fixed up for tourists to see. Or even like the Walter's mansion in Wisconsin. It was basically a big rectangle. At the top of the stairs I paused and tried calming my mind, opening it up to something, anything.

Nothing.

No Margaret.

No Norma.

Jo had entered one of the bedrooms and stood looking out of the front window toward the street. "Check this out. Dad is coming up here with Beth and your brother. Looks like Dad is letting them in. He's walking away. Wonder what they are up to?"

"Charlie said something about Halloween costumes this morning. Maybe they're looking for old clothes here?"

Jo got a wicked smile on her face. "Beth is always teasing me about why I want to visit a cemetery. I tease her that she's afraid to go there. She pumps up her chest and says she's not afraid of anything. How's about we try to make her prove that?" She put her finger up on her lips and tipped her head in one direction. I followed her as she hid behind a door.

We heard their voices downstairs and then squeaking steps as they came up. It sounded like they went in one of the other bedrooms. Jo tiptoed out into the hallway to peek. She waved me to follow. Shuffling along with our backs against the wall we headed toward the door of the room they were in.

Amy came out and looked up at us with her big brown eyes. She tilted her head and gave us a doggy smile. All the while her tail kept wagging. Jo tried to shoo her away, but she stayed.

I heard Charlie talking about what a great idea this was as Beth opened and closed drawers in the room. "Here are some old shirts. These should work," she said.

Charlie said, "Hey check out these caps."

Jo knocked on the wall.

Charlie and Beth stopped talking.

Jo stomped her feet slowly.

"Who's there?" Charlie said in a trembling tone.

"Dad," Beth said. "Is that you?"

Jo moaned in a long and low tone. "Help me. Someone help me."

I had to clamp my hand over my mouth to keep from laughing.

Charlie peered out into the hall, but we were hidden behind the door. "No one's out here. We should go find your dad," he murmured.

I couldn't make out what Beth said. Then everything went silent.

"BOO!"

Jo and I both screamed and jumped!

Beth and Charlie just stood there laughing at us. Amy

bent down over her extended front paws, ready to pounce and join the action.

"Told you I don't scare easy," Beth said. "What you guys doing here?

Jo said, "Looking for antiques for Mom. Maybe we'll find Halloween costumes too!"

Beth put her hands on her hips. "You don't go trick-or-treating anymore Jo Conner."

"Well I can change my mind little sister. Why are you here?"

"Same thing. Charlie is going to be a minuteman and I will be a hobo along with my trusty hobo buddy Amy."

Charlie and Beth walked back in the bedroom.

"Jeez, big sisters," Charlie said.

I heard Beth reply, "I know right?"

20

THE MYSTERY DEEPENS

Abigail listened as Meg explained what they knew about the mystery of the silver mirror. She finished going over the flyer information as best she could.

When she read the phone number at the bottom of the paper Abigail said, "I believe that phone number is based out of the United Kingdom."

Betty smirked. "And how do you know that?"

"My husband, God rest his soul, had some distant relatives in England. Every so often he'd pull out his special little address book and talk about calling them. I don't think he ever did. But I do vividly remember the country code being forty-four."

"There's an address on here too. It says Mr. Burgess can temporarily be reached at 289 Mill Street. That's got to be near us," Meg said. Her eyes looked up in a puzzled way. "I think that's the address of my dad's workshop. Or I guess it would be the house on the property. That can't be. No one lives there. And we have our friends from Kansas staying in the carriage house now so he couldn't be in there."

Betty said, "He probably just wrote it down wrong."

Flo nodded in agreement. "That's possible. But it's also possible he could be a ghost! We need a good ghost story here in Concord. He could be a British spy from the Revolutionary War period trying to trick us into turning over the silver vanity set."

Abigail chuckled, delicately covering her mouth. Betty looked over at her and snorted twice before bursting out in laughter. Flo looked at them both.

Flo said, "I don't get it. What's so funny?"

Betty leaned back in her chair. "You're setting us up for Halloween aren't you? Oooh ghosts and goblins oh my."

Indignant, Flo stood. "I believe in ghosts. What did you say this guy looked like Meg?"

Meg said, "I didn't see him."

"Well I'll bet he dressed oddly or spoke with a funny voice or some kind of ghostly giveaway. Like maybe he was super pale," Flo said, hands on her hips, stared down at Betty.

Betty looked Flo up and down. "Hmm, sounds like you're describing yourself Flo."

Abigail unsuccessfully tried to hide her giggle which prompted Betty to say, "See Abigail agrees with me."

Abigail frantically shook her head no as Flo said, "Well welcome to the club Abigail!"

"Club?" Abigail asked. "What club is that?"

"Oh girl, not a club. Just the two of us. But now that you've been added, we'll have to figure out a name."

Meg smiled. This was going well. Seems Betty realized that Abigail wasn't so uppity after all.

"Now that I'm in your club, will I get invited to happy hour at your place?" Abigail asked hopefully.

"Of course," Flo said.

"Ladies, can we get back to the mystery of this letter?" Meg asked.

"I'll bet it's a Halloween prank. Like a scavenger hunt your Mom is setting the stage for."

"I think I'd know about that," Meg answered dismissively. "I was going to say, Helen is the one who met him. She told Mom he was tall and thin. Dressed in, yes, old-fashioned clothes. Very British looking too."

"Did he wear a bowler hat like that guy walking across the street?" Abigail asked.

"And with a walking stick like his?" Flo added.

"OMG are we seeing a ghost?" Betty shouted.

The man tipped his hat to the ladies, causing them to giggle like school girls and wave.

"Ladies, listen," Meg laughed. "Seriously, he bought the mirror for a lot of money. He is offering a reward for information on the other pieces. It has these very distinct markings." Meg pointed out the details on the sketch. "See the initial? And the scrolls and vines and stuff?"

"There're millions of people with the last initial of P," Betty said.

"But it's a Paul Revere piece too, remember. That has to be valuable," Flo said.

Abigail sat silent. She was working hard to pick up all the information as everyone talked over each other.

Flo leaned in toward Abigail. "We all thought of you when we read about this. You are so classy looking and carry yourself so refined that we thought you were the most likely to have encountered such fancy things in your past life."

"Oh goodness," Abigail said.

Betty interrupted. "Where did your mother get the piece from? Who brought it into the shop to sell?"

Meg's brow furrowed. "I'm not sure. But now that you ask that, I'm thinking it came from the Peabody house. Might have something to do with the gentleman leaving that address."

"What's the Peabody house?" Flo asked.

"A house my dad bought. The last person to live there died decades ago, and the place was tangled up in her estate. No one could find the heirs. Eventually the state sold it for back taxes. All her possessions were left behind. Including the mirror Mom took to sell at her store."

Betty's eyes perked up. "Then the rest of the set must still be in there."

"I don't think so. Mom's been pulling out things to bring to sell at the shop so I would think she'd have noticed if it was part of a set."

Abigail had been silent.

"What is it?" Flo asked her.

"I believe I've seen a piece like in the sketch. I should get my reading glasses to look at it better. I wish I could see the actual mirror. It might help spark my memory."

"Maybe we should make a midnight trek to the haunted house and see if we can find that British guy and ask him about it," Betty said with a wink.

Flo laughed. "I always was a sucker for a British accent, so I'm up for it."

Abigail timidly raised her hand. "Me too please."

21

LILLIA

It startled me when Nate appeared at the top of the stairs.

"Ah...hi Dad," Jo said.

"Why are you here Jo? And how did you get in?" Nate asked.

"I know where you keep your extra key and I let us in the back door. Lillia wanted to see the house."

"Hello Mr. Conner," I said. "Sorry if we did something wrong."

"I don't mind you here at all. I wish you'd have let me know though. With Halloween right around the corner I want to make sure all the windows and doors are locked up tight tomorrow. In fact, I came back in to remind Beth about doing just that. Some kids aren't out for candy but for mischief making on Halloween."

"Okay Dad, sorry. Is it all right if we explore the

house? I'm looking for antiques for Mom," Jo said.

"Sure honey. I've decided to sell the place so go ahead and take anything. I'm listing it with a realtor this afternoon."

"You're selling?" Jo's face dropped. "But you love this place. All the dreams you had about restoring it."

Nate turned away from her as he said, "Sometimes things just don't work out."

"Dad, we came here too because of something we read. A guy who bought an antique at the shop left information about where he could be reached. And the strangest thing was he left this house's address written on the flyer."

Nate dismissed Jo's comment by saying, "He probably mixed up street numbers. I'd appreciate it if you locked up behind your sister. I'm stuck on some bathroom remodeling for the next couple of hours." Nate's shoulders drooped as he turned and walked out.

Gosh, I wish I could help him. Jo seemed discouraged too. There had to be some way we could find out who might have lived here before and had the other silver pieces. I wonder how much the reward would be if we succeeded.

"Jo, we've got to help your dad. If we find the other pieces, we can get the reward for him and that'll help with the money he needs right?"

"He can't sell this house. It'll just break his heart. But I don't know what more we can do. Maybe you'll have an imagining about where the silver pieces are?"

"We can go back to the graves of Norma and Julie to see if we can find out more from them. I leave day after tomorrow. We have to try!"

"But for now, let's look around here. I don't think Mom would have overlooked a valuable antique like a silver comb or brush, but you never know."

Beth and Charlie were still going through things in one of the bedroom closets.

"You find a costume yet Charlie?" I asked.

He held up a shirt and a pair of old-style pants. "These, but they're kind of big for me."

Beth eyed the clothes. "It'll be all right. I'll help him duct tape them up so they don't fall off. Hey look here's a door in the back of the closet. Looks like it goes to a place under the eaves. Maybe a secret hideaway space!"

Amy was nosing around the opening too. She let out a bark. She wanted to check it out and followed Charlie and Beth as they bent down to enter the space.

Because I suspected my claustrophobia would kick in, I didn't join them. But I couldn't help but wonder if they'd find anything interesting. Maybe the boy who slept in this bedroom long ago, used it to store his treasures?

22

MAKING CONNECTIONS

Meg was home for the evening working on the special task she'd been asked to do.

She still couldn't believe how Flo and Betty got along so well with Abigail right off the bat. They were a hoot to listen too. And that Abigail! Who'd have thought she was such a goof? Funny how people form an impression of someone and they can have it so wrong.

Earlier, before Meg had ended her work day at Maple Ridge, she learned a couple of other things.

First it turns out that when Abigail put on her glasses to have a better look at the sketch, she remembered seeing something similar. She thought it might be in one of her husband's memory boxes tucked away in the back of her hall closet. Packed away since their move back to Concord.

BRENDA FELBER

Second thing happened over a glass of evening wine with Flo and Betty. Abigail recalled the name of someone who might be associated with the vanity set. A distant relative of her husband who she'd met with a number of times.

Betty caught up with Meg before she left for home and pleaded with her. "I know it's a reach, but would you mind taking the name and doing a quick search on that Gaggle? Or Face Look?"

Meg didn't bother to correct Betty's terms for Google and Facebook but agreed to help. So here she was on her laptop, trying to find any information she could about the woman. She was narrowing it down when her mom came walking into the room to look over her shoulder.

"How was work tonight, honey?"

"It was so fun. I told three of the residents about the mirror mystery and the British stranger. They want to help solve it. Mom, you got that mirror out of the house Dad bought, right? The women would like to see inside the place."

"Yes, that's where it came from. Do they want to buy the place? I wish someone would take it off our hands pronto!"

Meg hated hearing her mother talk with that tone in her voice. She knew Mom wasn't happy with the way the house was draining their money. But Dad loved that place.

"Today Beth was in there with Nora's great-nephew Charlie digging around for Halloween costumes. Well at least we'll save a couple of bucks by not buying a costume for her," Mandy said.

"And the mirror was sold. That's good right?" Meg asked.

"Yeah sure. Goodnight…and don't stay up too late." Mandy shrugged and turned to leave but stopped. "Meg, I'm proud of how you are working so hard at Maple Ridge. You have a special connection with the elderly."

"Thanks. Night Mom."

Meg sighed. She turned back to her online search. This might not lead to finding the woman Abigail remembered or to the missing vanity piece either. But you never know. Maybe it was meant to happen. Abigail could get the reward and buy glasses and hearing aids.

Kitty was relaxing. She loved the fall months in Arizona when the blistering summer heat faded, and the days held a more comfortable temperature. Plus, an Arizona sunset like the one she was watching reflecting off the Superstition Mountains, couldn't be beat.

Each year she promised herself she'd visit Concord again. The autumn leaves were amazing there. But the years went by without it happening. She laughed thinking of how she had to practice *carpe diem* and seize the day!

Putting her crossword down she decided to check email on her tablet. She kept up with techie stuff because of her natural curiosity. Plus, it was how she stayed in touch with her far flung friends.

A Facebook message waited for her to open. She read it and responded. After a few exchanges of information. she was soon chatting with a young lady from Concord.

This felt like serendipity! She'd just been thinking about Concord.

When the girl, Meg Conner, brought up Abigail a lightbulb went off. But it was the mention of the engraved vanity set that really caught her attention.

Kitty remembered visiting with her distant cousin Joseph and his wife Abigail. She didn't want to fall prey to some internet scam, so she asked the girl, Meg, to describe Abigail.

Meg said, "She is very pretty and has her hair styled just so. She is very careful about her appearance and never is without her choker necklace of pearls."

Abigail told Meg that her description was spot on.

That was her cousin Joe's wife. Always dressed so proper like. No capris for her.

The conversation went back to the reason for the call and Kitty said, "I have a comb given to me by my great-grandmother many years ago. She claimed it came from a woman in our family who had moved to America when she was a young bride. I remember her talking about our British ancestry but I'm afraid I either didn't listen carefully or can't remember much of the story."

After ending the call, Kitty explored options. She found the comb and it fit the description perfectly. She sent a photo of it to Meg. And then the thought of why not enjoy a Massachusetts fall hit her.

Carpe diem!

Kitty contacted her travel agent to make arrangements to visit Concord. It had been too long since she did something so spontaneous and fun. She texted Meg the trip information but asked her to keep it a secret. She wanted to surprise Abigail.

23

LILLIA

I sat on our little second-story porch again tonight. I still couldn't sense if Concord would be good for ghost tours, probably because I was getting distracted by the mystery surrounding the mirror.

Tomorrow, being Halloween, might be a bust too because of all the fake little ghosts and wicked vampires stalking the streets with their plastic pumpkin treat buckets.

Oh well, I would keep my eyes and ears open and see how it goes. Guess that's the best I can do.

My thoughts drifted back to the Peabody house. Why did the British man leave this address as a place to contact him? Was it a clue?

The house didn't give up any information this afternoon. It feels like I'm missing something though. Something at the edges of my mind still flitting around. Will anyone ever be able to find the complete silver vanity set? How much is the reward? Would it be enough for Jo's family to keep the house?

Above me the stars revealed themselves one by one. Thin wisps of clouds drifted across the moon. Looking up at the night sky, I said out loud, "Grandpa, you got any ideas? I could use some help here."

A crisp rustling sound startled me. A dark figure stepped out of the shadows below me. At first I thought it might be Jo's dad coming to his work shop again.

"Mr. Conner, is that you?" I asked in a quavering voice.

"No Lillia Pameroy." A tall slim man stepped further into the dim light the moon supplied. He tapped his walking stick down with one hand and with his other hand took his round hat off, sweeping it across his chest as he bowed. "I am James Burgess. At your service."

"Mr. Burgess? Mr. Burgess! The man who bought the silver mirror?"

"That I am my dear lass."

"I'll be right down." I raced down the stairs.

He was gone! No!

Frantically I looked around. "Please come back."

"I'm right here dear."

"Where? I can't see you."

"Oh dear me. Forgive my manners. This has been a rather trying day."

His form shimmered back into view. He stood in a different spot. "I haven't been doing this regularly enough I fear. You see, I am your spirit guide here in Concord. However, there are so very many conflicting things pulling on me that it wearies a man's soul and tasks his powers."

"My spirit guide? I'm happy to meet you! But wait, you bought the mirror and left the information about the reward. Am I mixing things up here?"

"Fear not Lillia, you are not mixing things up as you say. My buying the mirror is part of my reason for being here."

He seemed like such a nice man. "I'm sorry you're having such a difficult time. I hope I'm not causing your troubles."

"Certainly not young lady." He took a deep breath and did a dramatic shoulder roll. "I'm ready to carry on. Chin up, cheerio, and all that."

Then, straightening his posture, he continued speaking. "Ah there. Much better. I am here to expedite the process of bringing together Margaret Peabody's silver vanity set once again."

"Oh hooray. So are we! The note said there is a reward. Do you know anything about that?" I asked him.

"Why yes I do," Mr. Burgess paused and shifted his stance. I could see he was trying to compose himself before continuing. "The offer of a reward arose in the hopes that a law firm, searching for the heirs of a British citizen lost at sea, could settle his estate. Please excuse my unkind words, but in my opinion they are simply daft!"

"That doesn't sound good."

He shook his head. "It's not! Their so-called search has been going on for over two centuries. I suspect they've been collecting fees the entire time. When it came to our attention you would journey to Concord, Massachusetts, the last known residence of Mrs. Peabody, I was sent as a spirit guide to be of help."

I was still absorbing the information he'd passed on. This was exciting! I had some help. "Jo and I sure can use your help to find the missing pieces."

He chuckled. "I am afraid I cannot be of direct help with that."

I must have let out a disappointed sigh because Mr. Burgess added. "Oh my, don't be discouraged. I believe you have done a great deal already. You are here to help pull things together for this fine old lady and me." He pointed up at the Peabody house. "She's been waiting a long time."

"I am? She has?"

"You must understand that I needed you for my presence to occur. No one else could have seen the image of Margaret in the mirror. You began it!"

"So that was her! I was right."

"I think there are people in the house tonight you might enjoy seeing. The front door is unlocked for you. Cheerio!" He turned and walked away down the path to the cemetery.

I raced after him for a short way, but he was gone. "Goodbye Mr. Burgess," I called softly before turning back to face the house.

I walked around toward the front and sure enough, the door was open. In fact, someone in a full skirted long dress had just entered ahead of me. I followed her into the house. In the parlor a hearth fire warmed the room.

"Welcome Lidian. What a chill in the air tonight. Come, sit by the fire with me. Mr. Thoreau and I were just talking about how things are going for him at Walden." On a floral covered settee sat a woman wearing a long black dress with a delicate white lace collar.

I thought she said Lillia, but no, she was talking to the woman who had entered ahead of me.

"Always a warm welcome in the Peabody home. You're looking wonderful my dear Victoria," Lidian said.

On the other side of the fireplace sat a young man. Unruly hair and a scraggly beard surrounded his weather burnished cheeks. "Good evening Mrs. Emerson. I hope you are well."

Lidian turned to speak to him. "I am well Mr. Thoreau, thank you for inquiring. However, I fear you will soon face the bitterness of a hard winter in your little cabin. Its arrival is in the air tonight. For the life of me I cannot fathom what you hope to achieve by this isolation you have imposed on yourself."

"I love the solitude Mrs. Emerson. I am eternally grateful to your kind husband for offering me the use of his property on Walden Pond."

"Our pleasure, but I am uncertain what it is you are hoping to achieve." Lidian turned back to Victoria. "Well my dear, I hope you have received word from your daughter. It sounds like she and her new husband are off on quite an adventure out West."

I watched Victoria carefully fold her hands around a handkerchief in her lap.

Who was she? She must be a Peabody. If this is the era of Thoreau, it has to be the 1800s according to his grave marker.

"Thank you for asking. It's been months now and I get the occasional letter, but I fear we'll not see them this year. I hope they can return for a visit next year...or the year after." She raised the white hankie to dab her eyes.

"There now, I didn't want to make you sad."

I watched a man come down the staircase and enter the room.

"She's right Mother. Don't be sad. They are pioneers now! Headed for faraway lands. It meant so much to my sister that you gave her the two pieces from Grandmother Margaret's vanity set. Now every night when she brushes her hair, she'll think of us. And again in the morning when she combs it to prepare for the new day."

I smiled. Now I knew why my spirit guide sent me here. I heard clues about the comb and the brush.

Victoria's face beamed. "Ah, you are right son. That is a good thought to keep in my mind. You are my sweet child."

"Please Mother, I'm hardly a child. In fact George, your beloved first grandchild, is already sweet on a young girl. He's growing up too fast."

"One of the Alcott girls? Is it Meg?" Henry Thoreau asked. "They seem to chum together. In fact, they visited me at Walden yesterday."

"Oh my no. He's sweet on little Julia from next door."

I know Julia! The Julia whose headstone Jo had been getting whispers from and was writing a story about.

Thoreau said, "Come on old man. What do you say we finish piling up that load of firewood that the Hawthornes dropped off earlier? If the weather is as bad as Mrs. Emerson implies, your family will need every bit of it this winter."

"I'll be leaving now too dear friend," Lidian said. "The snow is worsening I'm afraid."

Victoria walked her to the door. "I believe I'll join the men and help with the firewood."

While Lidian put on her cape, Victoria reached for a red plaid cloak to drape over her shoulders.

"I've always admired that cloak Victoria. It is made of such lovely fabric."

"Why thank you, it belonged to my late mother-in-law Margaret. I feel like she is still with me when I wear it."

The imagining faded away...

I was left standing in a room that slowly returned to the present. But on the coat tree hung a red plaid cloak. I reached out to touch it, fearful it would slip away too. It was damp from snowflakes still clinging to it.

24

CHARLIE'S DREAM

Charlie woke from his dream, but he kept his eyes closed, trying to keep a thread of the dream in his head. Just enough to hold on to and take him back in. That's how Grandpa had told him to do it. Pull the threads he always said.

In his dream someone had come walking into the backyard from the path that went to the Sleepy Hollow Cemetery. It was dark and he couldn't see who the person was.

Then what happened?

Charlie pulled on the next thread and remembered that he slipped behind a shrub, afraid of who was there. It was someone his own age, looking all around the yard. He seemed sad and frantic.

Then the kid got all tangled up in the shrubbery. Just out of Charlie's reach.

Charlie struggled to get to him. They both were thrashing about trying to get out of the twisting branches. Wait! Stop! You're making it worse. I'll help you.

The thread snapped…

Charlie opened his eyes.

Could that be the boy whose room he had been in earlier today? Was that his little hideaway place where Charlie found treasures? And were those his clothes and wooden gun that Charlie would use for his Halloween costume?

That put him in mind of Halloween. He forgot his dream and got to thinking about his costume. It was perfect! He would have the wooden gun and put the file on the end for a bayonet look. Did minutemen have bayonets? Didn't matter, he would have one. He smiled. Halloween here I come!

A new photo slid across Grauntie's digital frame. Charlie saw it was of the tent that Matt put up by the Alabama swamp. Wow, I was scared out there that night. Such strange sounds.

Charlie knew Grauntie left the frame on at night instead of a night light. His fears of the dark were still with him. There was just enough light to show him that

Lillia wasn't on the air mattress. He sat up and looked around the corners of the room.

Where was she?

In a low voice he called her name. The door to the bathroom was open. No one was there. Grauntie's door was shut.

He heard something outside.

Someone coming up the stairs.

Slowly the door knob turned.

He ducked under his blanket and peeked out, barely breathing. What was lurking outside the door?

25

LILLIA

I tried to be quiet as I opened the door to our apartment.

I hoped no one would wake up.

The lump under the blanket on the couch moved.

"What are you doing up Charlie? And why are you hiding?"

Charlie peeked out at me. "I was scared when I heard steps outside. Why are you wandering around this late?"

"I couldn't sleep so I was sitting on the deck."

He threw the blanket off. "Liar liar pants on fire! I heard you walk up the stairs. Where were you?"

"Chill! I went downstairs for a little bit. Go back to sleep Charlie."

"You'll stay here now? You won't go out again tonight?"

"Did you have a bad dream?" I knew Charlie didn't like the dark and had some doozy dreams.

Charlie nodded at me.

"I promise I'm in for the night. Go back to bed."

I slipped into my t-shirt and pajama bottoms. Looking at my reflection in the bathroom mirror I asked, "How do you even imagine you can find the brush and comb that went with someone who left to live out West?"

Then I answered myself, "Mr. Burgess says the vanity set mystery is why he came to me. That should mean something right?"

I nodded. "Right."

Enough talking to yourself, get to bed.

Lying down on the air mattress I tried to remember every moment of the imagining I'd just had in the Peabody house so I could share it with Jo tomorrow.

James Burgess was right about meeting people in the house. My imagining showed me Henry David Thoreau and Mrs. Ralph Waldo Emerson for one thing. Which was pretty cool! But that was just a part of it.

26

BACK IN TIME

One hundred years ago…

Anthony knew Mother was sick, but not that she was dying. Since she had taken ill, Anthony often found himself sleeping in the little space off his closet. It felt safe there. He felt protected.

Tonight it was raining. He liked the sound of the drops on the roof above him. They lulled him, comforting him, taking him out of the scary world that was pushing in on him. The worse his mother looked and the more weight she lost, the more he sought an escape in his secret room.

The hideaway place held all his treasures and pushed the bad things away. His yo-yo stayed with him during the day, but other more childish toys he still treasured were in here. A wooden rifle his great-grandfather had once carved. A toy drum his grandfather had played with as a boy. The Tangle Tales, a book signed by the author Nathaniel Hawthorne to his own father George Peabody.

He heard a knocking. He kept his eyes closed. Go away.

But she didn't.

Now she was pushing open the small door to his hideaway.

He kept his eyes closed. Go away.

But still she was there. He could feel her.

"Anthony? Come out of there right now."

He opened his eyes. Light from the room behind her outlined her shape. He couldn't make out her face. He feared what she had to say.

"Mother's taken a turn for the worst. You best come and sit with her for a spell."

"But it's late. Isn't she sleeping?"

"Anthony, come out of this childish little secret space right now. We must be strong for mother.

"She mustn't die yet. We have family coming to see her. Don't we? She has to wait for them."

"I don't think anyone's coming. You know it's always been just the three of us."

"What about our aunt? The one who lives far away? Can't she come? She would know what to do."

"Well it appears not. God is calling Mother home. Now pull yourself together. I was your age when Father died. I had to learn to grow up fast."

Anthony's eyes began tearing up. He trembled and his chin quivered.

"She has something she wants to give to you." Norma reached for her brother's hand and led him across the hall to her mother's room.

Anthony could hardly make out Julia Peabody's thin figure under the family quilts covering her.

Julia saw her son standing in the doorway. She took a deep breath, pushed the pain down, and smiled at him.

"Come closer Anthony my sweet boy." Her fingers lying outside the covers tapped lightly. "Come sit here by me. My goodness but you grow an inch every day."

Anthony sat on the edge of her bed. His mother held something that she lifted toward him.

"I want you to have this. It belonged to your great-great-grandmother Margaret Peabody. A strong and determined woman." She took three shallow breaths. "She raised your great-grandfather all on her own."

Again she struggled for breath, and in a weaker voice continued. "Margaret received a vanity set as a wedding gift. The pieces have been passed down in this family. Now this one is yours."

Norma reached for a cool cloth. As she leaned past Anthony she snapped, "Take it."

Gently she patted her mother's brow. "Thank you for giving me the mirror Mother. We'll treasure these heirlooms forever."

Anthony Peabody took the silver handled nail file from his mother. He choked back a sob.

"Don't be sad. I will always be with you two in spirit."

Anthony leaned down to whisper in his mother's ear. "Please don't go." He blinked quickly to push back his tears.

"I love you son," Julia said. She sunk deeper into the feather mattress.

"I love you Mother."

Norma ushered him out of Julia's room and left him standing in the hall.

It didn't take him long to begin sobbing. What were they to do without Mother? Would Norma be able to take care of the house? Would she take care of me?

He stumbled back to the comfort of his little hideaway place. And that is where he spent the night with the silver handled file clutched in his hand.

. . .

Now…

The Peabody house warmed in the Halloween morning sunshine. Her boards absorbed the sun's rays, storing them against the cold winter winds that were coming.

Inside the rooms were quiet. But last night she had welcomed visitors from her past. Things were stirring. Stories revealed. Truths uncovered.

The front steps accepted the simple paper-wrapped package delivered by the tall thin man and heard him say, "It appears hopeful that things are on the precipice of turning out well for us. And right on Halloween day too!"

He patted her boards and chuckled to himself, shaking his head side to side. "We are almost done old gal."

He stepped out to the sidewalk and turned his face up to the warming sun.

27

LILLIA

I looked out our kitchen window watching for Jo. The morning sun beams blinded me. I had so much I wanted to tell her. Meeting Mr. Burgess, the imagining in the parlor of the Peabody house, and that two of the pieces left Concord.

There she was. I dashed outside, down the steps and met her on the narrow little driveway.

Jo was holding a package in her hand. "This was left at the front door. It's addressed to the owner of 289 Mill St., Concord, Massachusetts. Guess that would be Dad. I'll leave it in his workroom for him."

Soon we were on our way to the cemetery. I explained about meeting James Burgess last night.

"The man who bought the mirror? Are you serious? What did he look like?"

"He was British. Tall, thin, very proper. Except he seemed stressed out a little. He sort of faded in and out."

"What? Faded in and out?" Jo said. "Lillia Pameroy, you are being a tease! Out with the truth."

I gave her a scrunched up little grin. "Well I learned that buying the mirror and looking for the other pieces isn't the only thing Mr. Burgess is in Concord for. He's my spirit guide too."

"Your what? Come on Lillia, seriously, help me out here. What is a spirit guide?"

"I'm not sure, but they sort of hang around to see how I'm doing."

Jo said, "So this fading guy is not real? He's a ghost?"

"He's as real as the whispers you hear."

Jo kept walking but I knew she was trying to put this all together. "But different, because Helen at the shop saw him. She described him. So now she can see ghosts or what?"

"I'm still not sure how my imagining stuff works. Or how spirit guides help. I've had real people see them before though. Like the one named Mairead in Alabama. She took a whole pirate tour cruise with us, everyone on board saw her. All I know is that last night Mr. Burgess told me to go in the Peabody house to meet someone."

"Wow! Who was it?"

This was moving so fast. I didn't want Jo doubting

my story. I couldn't throw all of it at her at once. I could tell that she was having a hard time wrapping her mind around what I was telling her.

Jo grabbed hold of my arm and shook it. "Lillia Pameroy, don't you dare hold back on me now." Then she softly punched my shoulder. "We're in this together remember?"

"Ouch!"

"Sorry, but you can't keep things from me."

Okay I thought, here goes. "I met some of the Peabody family! Can you believe it? Best I can figure it was Margaret's daughter-in-law Victoria. Maybe we'll be able to confirm that today at the cemetery."

Jo pondered a moment, then said, "So what's the deal with Burgess buying the mirror then? Can't he tell you where the other pieces are?"

"Spirit guides tell me they have limited knowledge of the mystery I'm supposed to solve. Or the truth I'm supposed to uncover. Like last night I got another clue about the vanity set," I said.

"What did you find out?"

"She gave the brush and comb to her daughter who moved out West with her husband."

Jo's shoulders sagged "So all we still have is the mirror."

"Remember, we don't have the mirror. James Burgess does."

"OMG you're right. We don't even have the mirror. We have none of the pieces!"

28

SELLING THE HOUSE

Back in Concord preparations for the annual Halloween pumpkin fest and costume parade were being completed. This annual celebration was a favorite of the citizens of Concord as it drew in people from the surrounding area and lent a local and festive air to the town.

Carved pumpkins held candles waiting to be lit when evening's darkness descended. Candy was placed in bowls, bags or ghoulish containers to pass out to the ghosts and goblins who would appear later in the day.

The Conner house was ready for Halloween. Though not on a main street, Mandy always welcomed any little trick-or-treaters. She dressed in her witch costume and played spooky music.

But all that would come later. Now she was planning

a day of site seeing with Nora Pameroy. It was always a delight to show off Concord to tourists. The Orchard House was their first planned stop.

With her love for all things Alcott, the place made her feel good and she could use a pickup. Yesterday she had insisted Nate put the house up for sale. Who knows how long it will take to sell. With winter coming she held little hope of it happening this year, but maybe by spring. She was tired of all the family tension and looked forward to enjoying a day with Nora.

Beth came bounding downstairs and headed out the front door.

"Hey there little one, where are you off to?"

"Meeting Charlie. We're finishing putting our Halloween costumes together."

"So, no zombie scarecrow again? What are you going to be?"

"We found tons of old kids' clothes at the Peabody house. Charlie will be minuteman and Amy and I are going to be hobos."

"How did you get in the house?"

"Dad opened it up for us. Jo and Lillia were there too. Gotta run Mom."

That's odd Mandy thought. What was everyone doing there?

I'd better go over too and scour the place for anymore antiques that might sell she thought as she grabbed her car keys.

* * *

Meanwhile Nate was meeting with a realtor to start the process of selling the Peabody house. He hated to do it, but he had to admit that Mandy was right. Their family finances just couldn't support carrying his dream any longer.

The realtor was optimistic even though the place had sat vacant so long. She suggested Nate share his ideas for the house with future buyers.

"Maybe you'll even get the job of remodeling it for someone," she said in a chirper voice. "It would make a great historical rental for someone wanting to experience living in a historic saltbox style home."

Nate said, "Sure. That's a possibility." But it broke his heart. He didn't want to fix her up for someone else. He had dreamt so long of the bed and breakfast idea that it was hard to imagine it any other way.

"I'll write up the contract for you to sign later. Do you mind if I put my sign up right away?"

Nate said, "Go ahead."

His spirit was broken, but life goes on. At least Mandy will be happy about getting rid of it. He walked out to his pickup and drove back to the house he was remodeling.

29

LILLIA

I finished telling Jo about last night as we walked through the cemetery toward Julia Peabody's headstone. "Since I shared so much with you, tell me more about how you listen for the stories?"

"Like I said before, I came here because I liked the feeling of the place. It's not spooky or sad. It's peaceful. Everything is still and calm here. I can write in the quiet of nature."

"Sounds very Thoreau-like," I said.

Jo smiled. "You might be right. In fact, one time I was walking around on the Author's Ridge and my back was to the Thoreau family plot when I heard whispers."

"So, you wrote a story given to you by Thoreau?"

"No, but I wish he would."

"How did you get the story you gave me to read?"

"I was here trying to make up a story about the house Dad had bought. I was trying to imagine who had built it. Who had lived there? I was working on a story about a man who built it for his family when a low female voice said *if you want to know the truth, sit by me awhile.*"

"Which grave was that whispering coming from Jo?"

"It was Norma Peabody's. Come on I'll show you." She motioned me toward a small hill nearby. "There's another one next to it that you'll want to see too. One I should have shown you earlier."

I followed her. Jo stopped by an ancient headstone. I could barely read the name and dates on it.

She pulled out a paper and pencil from her backpack and dropped to her knees in front of the headstone. Holding the paper over the etched letters, she angled the pencil tip and rubbed lightly back and forth across the paper.

I watched these letters appear...

Margaret Burgess Peabody
B:1752, Lancaster, England
D:1843 Concord, Massachusetts, USA

Jo stood. She handed me the paper saying, "This is the woman who built the house. The woman who owned the Paul Revere silver vanity set."

I couldn't believe it. "You knew this and didn't tell me? I thought we were partners."

Jo nodded, her eyes downcast.

I felt hurt. Betrayed. I had told her everything, but she hid the fact that Margaret's maiden name was Burgess.

"So, when we sat on the bench that day and you read the flyer with me, you knew?"

Jo looked up. Her eyes pleaded for forgiveness. "I'm so sorry."

"Why didn't you tell me? I thought we trusted each other."

"Please Lillia, forgive me. I'm so confused. One day I'm Jo Conner sitting in the graveyard and happy as a clam writing my stories about the people buried here. I could pretend I wasn't hearing whispers because that would make me crazy. Right? And then you come along. You see dead people. Are we both crazy?"

I knew how hard living with a paranormal ability could be. After all, when my mother found out about me, she feared me. She still does.

I took Jo's face in both my hands and looked her in

the eyes. "I've known others. And now you know me. We are not crazy."

I gave her a hug and said, "Now let's build a Peabody family tree and see if we can figure this out."

Jo hugged me back and whispered, "Thank you."

It seemed unbelievable. Mr. Burgess related to Margaret Peabody? Wow!

We spent the next hour looking at graves. Jo knew where some of the other Peabodys were buried. We wrote down dates and started getting what looked to be a family tree.

The tree had one very short limb though. We found the grave of Anthony Peabody. He had died at the age of sixteen.

"By the year on here, he must have been Julia's son, the boy who slept in the room Charlie and Beth were in yesterday," Jo said.

"And maybe Norma's brother?" I asked.

30

GATHERING PIECES

"You found her! I can't believe it. You're the best," Abigail said.

Flo held up two fingers. "And now two pieces down, two to go."

"Three if you count the mirror that British guy bought at the store," Meg added. She was happy for them. And couldn't wait for Kitty's surprise arrival later today.

"We should see if we can get the reward without the fourth piece," Flo said.

Beth snorted. "Yeah sure. They'll go for that."

Abigail said, "I'm so glad you found Kitty. My husband died shortly after he moved us to Concord. So, I figured end of story. All this newfangled techie stuff is something else. Maybe you can give some lessons on it Meg?"

"Not a bad idea. I could start a class right here at Maple Ridge. But, tell me more about the silver brush you found last night. Was it just something in his stuff?" Meg asked.

"I knew it was a family heirloom. I was planning to give it to my daughter one day. But goodness, if we can put the set back together and get a reward…" She looked embarrassed, she wanted no one's pity over her financial situation.

"What's that old bumper stick we used to see on cars. I'm spending my kids' inheritance?" Flo said. "That will be you Abigail."

Betty said, "It's all right. We all would like extra spending money. I'm sure your daughter wouldn't mind if you gave it up for a reward."

Abigail looked relieved. "You might be right. Whenever I ask if there's anything of mine, she wants I get these funny looks before she says I'm good Mom, but thanks anyway."

"I'll see if we can get in the Peabody house. Are you up for digging through old stuff?" Meg asked.

"Oh, an adventure!" Abigail clapped her hands.

"I'm in!" Flo cheered.

"For sure!" Betty shouted.

The group all high-fived.

Meg said, "But tonight's Halloween. Okay if we do it tomorrow?"

Flo said, "My motors running right now. Can't we head over there?"

Betty said, "Trick-or-treaters will be out soon. Can't miss that. What if the reward is only $100?"

Meg said, "But imagine if it's $100,000!"

Abigail's eyes teared up. If not for these new friends I won't have even known about the reward she thought.

"Meg, why did your Dad buy the house anyway?" Flo asked.

"He wanted to turn it into a bed and breakfast. But now I think he's gonna sell it. Could never get the time or money together to finish it up."

Flo stood and announced, "I say you buy the place Abigail and hire him to restore it. Then we can all live there together."

Abigail's eyes popped wide open, and she gasped. "Oh yes! Perfect!"

Meg said, "Ah what if there's no big reward?"

"I say we put on disguises and do a bank heist." Betty pointed to the First National Bank across the street. "That one! No one would suspect three old broads. We'd tuck the money in our clothes, slip out the back, and sit in our rockers before they sound the alarm. And then when the police question us, we'd be all like, gosh no, we saw nothing officer."

"I want to be a flamingo dancer for my disguise," Flo said.

"I claim hop hop or broke dancer or whatever those guys with the saggy pants are called," Betty said.

Meg stopped laughing long enough to ask Abigail, "What would you be?"

Abigail pursed her lips and raised her nose in the air. "Why I would be a prima ballerina of course!"

Across town Mandy and Grauntie Nora were touring the Alcott home, Orchard House. They had walked through the kitchen, Bronson Alcott's study, and the parlor before they entered the dining room.

"Isn't this an amazing treasure for us to see? Most of the furnishings here belonged to the Alcott's," Mandy said. "And in this room, I can just feel what their weekly open houses must have been like. The girls performing their plays or playing music. The people who must have passed through here and the things they discussed."

"I can't tell you how much it means to see something in this condition. I didn't realize the house is well over

350 years old. And that it sat here on Lexington Road when the British marched through. Quite amazing."

"It was during the Civil War period that the Alcott's lived here. They were staunch abolitionists. Imagine the discussions held around this dining room table."

Nora said, "If these walls could talk! I wonder the same thing about the Peabody house...what those walls have seen. When was that built?"

"I'm not sure. But whatever, we're selling it. The sooner the better," Mandy said. "Someone else can listen to its stories. Let's head upstairs."

"Oh yes! I want to see Louisa May's little writing desk. You must be so proud of your Jo and her writing."

"I am Nora. I know she's enjoyed spending time with Lillia. Did she find anything about ghost tours for Tiffany?"

"I don't think ghostly things were as obvious as she had hoped. We haven't talked much about it. In fact, she's spent most of her time with Jo." Nora said. "There's a ghost tour of the Sleepy Hollow Cemetery tonight. Maybe the girls would like to go with me."

"Jo asked me about that too. Sounds like a good resource of what Concord offers ghost wise," Mandy said. "And here you go Nora, this is the desk Little Women was written at."

31

LILLIA

"I think we found good information today," I said.

"But not enough to figure out where even one piece of the set is," Jo said in a very frustrated voice. "Me and my big dreams to save the Peabody house for Dad."

"Do you want to search the house again?"

"Nah, I doubt we'd find anything."

"I'm so sorry Jo. I leave tomorrow. Maybe someone will contact the antique store with more information? Don't give up."

"I'm not holding my breath. It was fun while it lasted, but sometimes things just don't work out. No matter how much you want them to."

We emerged from the path into the back yard of the Peabody house. As we walked the narrow drive past the corner of the house, we were both startled to see a realtor's For Sale sign in the front yard.

"What's going on?" I asked.

Jo bit her lower lip and sadly shook her head side to side. "I felt something like this was coming. I hear Mom and Dad arguing. How the house is a money pit. That Dad will never get to finish it. That they can't keep paying taxes and heating it anymore."

There had to be something more I could do to help. Otherwise why did I see Margaret in the silver mirror? Or meet Mr. Burgess and learn about Victoria giving pieces to her children? It all had to mean something!

I'm here for more than helping Tiffany, Mr. Burgess told me so. "Jo, we have to go one more time. Our flight doesn't leave until late tomorrow. Please? One more time in the morning?"

"No, that's okay. But thanks for asking." Jo was walking away when she said, "Oh, I forgot to tell you, Mom told me there is a ghost tour in the cemetery tonight."

She sounded so down. I tried to cheer her up. "Hooray! Let's do that. I'm kind of sorry we won't be trick-or-treating though."

Jo kept on walking with her head down. "I was thinking about that..."

"I don't have a costume Jo. And maybe we're too old?"

She stopped and looked at me with an astounded expression. "Too old? Never! Come on ghost hunter girl. I've got ideas for our costumes and I have everything at the house."

"Yippee, candy stash here we come." I was happy to see Jo getting in a better mood. After all, it was Halloween.

Jo used black eye makeup pencils to draw cat eyes, whiskers and noses on us. She created pointy ears and tails out of black craft felt. We were just heading out, practicing our cat-like paw movements, when we ran into her mom and Grauntie coming back from their site seeing.

"Grauntie, we're going to the Sleepy Hollow haunted tour later. Want to come with us?"

"For sure! I just mentioned that to Mandy. You might get some more ideas for Tiffany from it, right Lillia?"

I said, "I sure hope so. Going trick-or-treating in town for a little bit right now. Catch up with you later?"

Mandy said, "Nora, why don't you meet up with the girls at the Maple Ridge Village? I know Beth plans on being there with Charlie too. She says kids get the best candy from those grandmas and grandpas."

32

HALLOWEEN

Main Street was busy. Music of a witchy mystical tenor floated out across the little ghosts and goblins, the scarecrows and cartoon characters, the superheroes and the princesses. Staff at shops and restaurants handed out goodies to the trick-or-treaters.

Among them were Beth and Charlie. They'd already done both sides of Main Street. Amy was getting tons of attention and doggy treats too.

They turned down the angled street that ran past the Maple Ridge Village. "My sister Meg told me we have to check it out. All the grandpas and grandmas are super generous with candies they give out," Beth said.

Charlie peered in his plastic pumpkin bucket. "I'm like half full already. And no apples for once!"

* * *

Kitty had arrived in Boston earlier and rented a car for her drive to Concord. Turning down the angled street, feelings of how right this felt swirled inside her. The monogrammed silver edged comb she carried with her was just part of it, the bigger piece was surprising Abigail. And on Halloween night? How fun!

The entrance to the old folks home Meg had directed her to appeared just as she slowed to let a soldier and a hobo with a dog cross the sidewalk in front of her. How cute are they?

Ahead sat a classic white clapboard two-story building. Black shutters hung on either side of multi-paned windows. A sign reading Welcome Center hung above the sidewalk.

This isn't a typical old folks home like I expected Kitty thought. Why I'd live here in a minute. Small cottages perched on walkways that meandered among trees. Costumed children roamed from cottage to cottage gathering goodies from the residents.

Kitty parked and walked up to the Welcome Center. Benches and light posts with cornstalks tied to them lined the way. She noted a nice looking man sitting on one of the benches, his hands resting on his upright walking stick. At first she thought he might be in costume, what with that bowler hat and out of date black suit, but as she got closer, he didn't seem to be. He dipped his head as their eyes met.

She saw three older women and a teenager on the expansive porch attached to the front of the welcome center. Okay, here we go. She walked toward them. Seeing a questioning look on the teen's face Kitty gave her a wink.

Casually and slowly Kitty walked toward the group. But before she got there the soldier and the hobo ran ahead of her and yelled, "Trick-or-treat!" Meg grimaced and held up her finger to Kitty.

Ten minutes later, Jo and Lillia approached the Maple Ridge Retirement Village. They searched for signs of Grauntie Nora.

Jo saw her sister Meg on the front porch, a group of ladies surrounding her. Everyone excited, talking over each other. Mixed in the group were Charlie, Beth and Amy.

"What is going on Meg?" Jo asked as she walked up.

"Exciting stuff. Hey everyone, this is my sister Jo." She pointed to Flo, Betty, and Abigail introducing them as part of the gang here at Maple Ridge.

"Yep that's us. The MRV gang," Betty said, flashing some crazy mix of hand signals. "I'm not sure what my hands just said!"

Meg said, "I don't think anyone does. And this is our surprise visitor, Kitty from Arizona."

"Surprise isn't the word for it Meg!" Flo said.

Betty added, "Tell her the rest of the story."

"Can I hear too," Grauntie Nora said as she joined everyone. "I love a good surprise."

"I don't know if Mom told you Jo, but there was something from her store that got sold and the person who bought is offering a reward for the missing pieces. And now we have two of them!" Meg said.

Abigail had her arm around Kitty. "I have one piece and my long lost cousin-in-law has one. Two more to go."

"Before you all get talking again, solving this woo-who big mystery we're taking off. We have two more streets to cover before dark. Come on Charlie," Beth said.

Raising his wooden rifle against his shoulder, Charlie did a soldierly turn. "See you back home."

"Hey, be careful with that rifle," Grauntie said, leaning back away from Charlie. "That pointed thing on the end looks dangerous!"

"Ha ha…this is my bayonet now!" Charlie said.

"I told him minutemen didn't carry bayonets," Beth said. "But he insisted they could have."

Lillia winked at Charlie and said, "Mere details?"

Charlie gave her a thumbs up before thrusting the wooden gun in the air. "On to freedom for America and more candy." He shouldered it and marched off, Amy prancing along behind him.

33

LILLIA

As I spun away to let Charlie parade by, I heard Jo say, "You have some of the vanity pieces? We were looking for them too!"

"Then you heard about it. Isn't it exciting?" Meg said. "Abigail here has the brush and Kitty the comb.

I was astonished. Here we were both about ready to give up on putting the set back together, and now we're standing next to ladies who own two of the pieces. Must be from the family that moved away long ago.

Jo asked, "Why did Mom give the flyer to you Meg?"

Betty said, "She probably gave it her because it involved antiques. And we're nothing if not antiques!"

Everyone burst out laughing, including Grauntie, who asked, "Why did Mandy give it you Jo?"

Jo said, "Because Lillia saw…"

I interrupted her. "I saw the mirror the day we got here. Remember when we went in the antique store? I saw the initial P on it. P for Pameroy!"

Jo leaned over and whispered. "Oops, I almost gave you away."

"And we've been trying to figure it out too because we both love a good mystery!" I added. I caught Grauntie giving me a *what's up?* look but thankfully she didn't say anything more.

"Kitty just offered to make a call to the English law firm seeing as she has that international calling on her cell phone," Betty said. "I still can't figure how those things work, but talking to someone in another country like that? I'm impressed!"

"Come on Kitty, make that call," Flo said.

We all leaned in as she dialed. Kitty put the phone on speaker so we could hear when the law firm answered. A recorded message said it was closed for the day. Kitty left a carefully worded message inquiring about the reward offered and left her phone number.

"This is hard to read. But it looks like there's an address in town. Why don't we contact him there?" Kitty asked.

I said, "That address is to the Peabody house. No one lives there. We figured he must have made a mistake with the house number."

Betty said, "Maybe they meant Old Mill Road?"

"Or Barretts Mill Road out east of town," Flo said.

"You two want to meet us at the Peabody house tomorrow morning?" Meg asked. "Since you're interested in this mystery too?"

"For sure," Jo and I both said at the same time!

Grauntie looked at her watch. "Come on my two little creepy cats, the tour of Sleepy Hollow will start soon."

34

THE PACKAGE

Nate was packing it in for the day. He had a few things to take to the workshop before he headed home.

Seeing the For Sale sign in front of the Peabody house hit him with a jolt. This was happening. The emptiness of the house made him sad. *Some things just aren't meant to be and my restoring this old gal is one of them.*

He remembered the first time he entered the house. Because Norma Peabody had died suddenly, everything was just like she left it. No one came to clean up or tend to her personal belongings. Dishes were still in the sink. Coffee had evaporated to a dark crust in the pot. A sweater hung from a kitchen chair. Boots stood on a mat by the front door.

Now the house just looked tired, kind of like me and this old pickup, he thought as he pulled tools from the bed of his truck to take to the workshop. Switching on the overhead lights with his shoulder, Nate stepped in. I should subdivide this carriage house from the big house when I sign papers tomorrow. Wouldn't mind hanging on to it.

He noticed a package left on his chair. It was addressed to the resident of 289 Mill Street. He sat down to open the brown paper package tied with a string. This is unusual he thought. Everything is sealed for shipping nowadays. Inside was a hand mirror made of gleaming silver. Beautiful design work was etched into the shiny surface.

Odd. Wonder where it came from? He put the mirror back down on the chair to return to stowing away his tools.

Would be a busy day tomorrow, but maybe he could finish up that project and get paid soon. He grabbed the package on the way out thinking he'd show it to Mandy when he got home.

Handling a call from a client distracted Nate on his short drive home. He forgot about the package.

35

LILLIA

I enjoyed listening to the stories of the tour guide at the Sleepy Hollow Cemetery. The voice he used was spooky. Low, pulling everyone in to hear better. And then he'd suddenly do a *did you hear that?* Or he'd snap his head, widening his eyes as though something startled him. He was a great storyteller, pointing to a grave, like Louisa May Alcott's, and then weaving a tale involving Orchard House.

He explained that this cemetery's parklike design was unusual for the times. He took us on an imaginary journey to the past, pointing out graves of people who had strolled these grounds at twilight. Transition from life to death seemed to blur and blend together.

"Can't you picture the ghosts that must still walk here

at night?" he said, "Returning to enjoy the place over and over."

Jo leaned over and said, "I'm thinking about some good ideas for Tiffany here. Plus, with what I could tell her, she'd do a great business! I can almost see those ghostly figures he's talking about."

I could see them. I was looking at one! She wore a red plaid cloak that hung below her knees. She stood near a tall narrow headstone, watching me.

I turned to find Jo. She had moved next to Grauntie, listening intently to the tour guide. I slipped away to approach the spirit.

As I walked in her direction she walked away, glancing back over her shoulder to confirm I was following her.

That cloak. I knew it. "Mrs. Peabody?" I whispered. "It's me Lillia."

She stopped. "You are the young girl who saw me in my mirror?"

"Yes I did."

"I'm so glad. Finally, someone to help us."

"Us?" I asked.

Margaret looked out across the moonlit cemetery. A gentle smile formed. "Me and the home I built and loved. She's looking rough wouldn't you say?"

"Well, she's seen better days I guess. What can I do? I

know that Nate is selling the house. Will someone buy it who can fix it up?"

"Oh no, Nate is the perfect owner of the house. He has the same passion for it I did when I built it. He just needs a little help. And that's where you come in."

"I don't understand."

"Lillia, when you picked up that mirror you opened a portal for my father to arrive. And things are building from there. I can't stay longer now, but I'm happy that I got to thank you in person."

She faded. Her cloak shifting, fibers slipping out of it and twirling away.

"Wait! Don't go!"

"Tomorrow..." was all she said before disappearing.

36

GATHERING PEOPLE

Morning in Concord found Mandy, Jo and Meg walking down Mill Street toward the Peabody house.

Flo, Betty and Abigail had piled into Kitty's rental car and were on their way to 289 Mill Street.

Nora and Lillia walked down the steps from their temporary home in the second floor of the carriage house and across the narrow drive.

When Mandy saw the For Sale sign on the front yard, she had to take a deep breath. She was feeling bad about giving Nate such a hard time these past weeks, but the sign was a punch in her gut. So he'd put it up for sale like she told him to do. This was really happening.

Last night Meg had explained what the Maple Ridge women discovered and how they wanted to see inside the house. She was here today to open it up for them.

When Nora saw Mandy she said, "Did you hear about the reward? When I met the girls at Maple Ridge last night, I walked into quite an excited group."

"Yes, Meg told me bits and pieces," Mandy said.

"Maybe they'll hear back from that law firm in England today. Look, here they are now."

"Good morning ladies. I'm Meg's mom," Mandy said as she walked up to shake hands with each of them.

Flo said, "I understand you sold the silver mirror that started this treasure hunt. One more piece to go! Between us we should find that last sneaky fingernail file. Why don't you show Mandy the pieces?"

"Did you bring your comb Kitty? I brought my brush," Abigail said as she reached in her purse and pulled out a soft blue fabric bag.

Kitty nodded and pulled out the silver comb tucked inside a clear plastic zip-lock bag from her purse. "I'm not as classy as you," she said with a laugh.

"Well, as I remember the mirror, those would be part of the same set. From what I'm understanding, Abigail and Kitty are related to the Peabody's of Concord." Mandy said.

"It would appear so, Kitty said. We talked about that last night and plan on researching our ancestry more. Maybe a trip to Lancaster is called for?"

"I'm going to go through more of my husband's

things and see if we can locate that British family he talked about," Abigail said.

Betty said, "Good for you two. But I say let's get on with finding that dang fingernail file. Come on ladies! Let's do this!"

Just then Nate pulled up in his old pickup. His surprise at seeing so many people walking into the Peabody house this early in the morning changed to dismay when he realized they might be buyers. He hadn't even signed the contract yet. The place couldn't go that quick!

He saw Mandy and called out to her. "What's going on?"

37

LILLIA

A bewildered looking Nate come in the house and joined us.

"I'm here to see that I didn't miss anything worth putting for sale in the antique shop. And these four ladies are looking for a finger nail file," Mandy said.

"A nail file?" Nate said, his eyes squinted with a puzzled look.

Betty laughed. "It's a long story."

"I see you're selling," Kitty said to Nate.

Abigail gasped, grabbing Kitty's arm and leaning in to say, "We don't have the reward yet. We don't even know how much it is."

Flo said, "And wait a minute. If the nail file is in the house, then it is owned by Nate. Wouldn't he get a cut of the reward?"

"What reward?" Nate asked. "What is going on here?"

Mandy shushed him and said, "I'll explain later."

"Oh for heaven's sake, would you all stop?" Betty let out a big sigh. "This is all well and good, but don't get too far out over your skis."

Kitty said, "She's right. Let's get this search started. I want to see more of this beauty of a house. Such classic lines. Nate, I understand you are a remodeler?"

"Yes, guess I am now. I used to consider myself more of a restorer. But restoration stopped paying the bills so now I do remodeling."

Jo said, "He's great at restoration work. And business will pick up again one day."

Nate gave Jo a hug. "Thanks sweetie. Someday I will get back to it."

"This place is a real gem Nate. What were you planning to do with it?" Kitty said.

Betty peered around into the parlor and walked back toward the kitchen. "I say you all spend the reward restoring this beauty. Make it a bed and breakfast. Flo and I will be your staff."

Abigail laughed. "Again, we're jumping ahead of things."

Nate looked surprised. "That was my plan! Do

updating like taking out this wall and exposing the stair-case to create more openness."

"That would be a fantastic idea. If it's a bearing wall, it would be easy enough to put a header across the stairs and conceal the support in a boxed column," Kitty said.

Impressed, Nate said, "My thought exactly. Where'd you learn about construction?"

"In my day I did a bit of building myself."

"If I remember the times we visited you, it wasn't so little. Don't I remember you doing a whole subdivision?" Abigail said. "Nate, I'd like to see what color scheme you were thinking of."

"I have samples in a project folder I could show you. I'd like to keep elements of the old colors and wallpaper treatments, but then merge them with some new focal points of color."

I watched as Abigail, Kitty and Nate gathered, talking excitedly about what they could do with the Peabody House.

Flo said, "My dear Betty Boo, it appears the dreamers are spending money they don't have.

Mandy laughed. "Nate loves talking about what he could do with this place. I'm off to search for more antiques to sell and maybe we can manage to save this old place."

"Did I hear Mom say maybe we could save this place?" Jo said, as Mandy walked away.

"She did!" I said.

"And we're off to look for that file. We can all dream!" Flo said. "Come on old lady, let's head up to the bedrooms and look for that last piece."

Betty joined Flo but stopped halfway up the stairs and said. "Hey you all, where is the mirror anyway?"

Everyone looked around at each other. No one spoke.

"I thought so. We have half of what's needed for the reward. Hopefully when you hear from that British firm they'll know where that Burgess guy is."

I knew where he was...in a way. But nothing I could tell Betty or Flo.

Nate turned to look up at Betty. He held up his hand. "Wait a minute. Did you say mirror?"

I jumped when Katy Perry's song Roar suddenly started playing.

38

THE CALL

"Excuse me." Kitty reached in and peeked at her cell phone screen. "It's them!" she shouted, scrambling to get the phone out and answer it. "Hello."

Betty just shook her head. "Isn't that the darndest thing? Here we are standing in a house in Concord, Massachusetts in the United States, and Kitty there picks up a gadget from her purse and is now talking to someone from Lancaster, England way across a big old ocean?"

"Shh…" Flo spit out. "Let her hear what they have to say."

"Oh my," Abigail whispered. "I'm so excited."

While the others stopped in their tracks, listening to one side of a conversation, Nate walked outside. He remembered the package he'd found yesterday in the workshop. The mirror. Could it be what they were talking about?

He got it out of his old pickup.

Kitty was still listening to whoever was on the other end of the call. An occasional *yes* or *correct* was all she said in response. A small nod of her head and an *ooh* escaped her lips. She kept listening as she took in her audience. Betty and Flo stopping on the staircase. Abigail bouncing with anticipation. Mandy and Nora watching with inquisitive tilts to their heads. Meg, Jo and Lillia leaning in to hear.

"Yes I will do that." Pause. "Of course. Whichever way you think best." Kitty smiled encouragingly at everyone. "Oh really? Well that's wonderful!" She gave a thumbs up. "I'll text you my email address right now and we can begin the process." She paused before saying, "That's great. I'll be in touch. Thank you for getting back to me so promptly." She ended the call.

Quiet.

Knowing that everyone waited, she teasingly typed a message on her phone screen.

"For heaven's sake woman, what did they say?" Betty broke the silence.

Kitty looked up with a smile.

"Don't make us wait? Is there a reward?" Abigail asked.

Kitty smiled. "Well…" She clicked her phone off and returned it to her purse, before answering, "Yes that's part of it."

"Woot toot!" Betty said.

Nate came back in with a paper-wrapped bundle. Jo recognized it as the one she found by the front door yesterday.

He held it out for everyone to see.

"What's that Nate?" Mandy asked.

"A package I found in my workshop. It's addressed to the owner of the house. I opened it but didn't know what it was about, so I put it in my truck figuring I'd ask you about it. Then I forgot to bring it in last night."

I remembered the package. Jo had found it at the front of the house and put it in her dad's workshop before we walked to the cemetery yesterday. I felt a shiver run through me.

Nate unwrapped the brown paper to reveal the mirror I had seen in the antique shop the day I arrived. Only now it was bright and shiny!

I had a flash of those few seconds of imagining over again. I remembered that on the shoulders of the last image of Margaret, I saw the red plaid cloak that was now hanging on the coat tree behind Nate. The same cloak she'd worn at the cemetery last night.

Nate raised the mirror so everyone could see it. But my attention went to what was going on behind him. I watched the cape lift off the coat tree and move out the open front door. Inside it the shape of a woman took form. She walked away from the house and as she got to the sidewalk Mr. Burgess, in his bowler hat, joined her. They linked arms and strolled away down the sidewalk among the scattered fall leaves.

It was in those seconds between Mr. Burgess and Margaret walking and me losing sight of them I heard happy screaming filling the air.

"Guess this is the mirror you're looking for?" Nate said in a dry voice with just the hint of a smile.

"Are you kidding me?"

"Where did you get that?"

I watched as Abigail took the mirror and moved to show it to the others. "It matches my brush. This is part of the set!"

I realized that Kitty hadn't told us what the people in Lancaster told her.

Jo elbowed me and gave me a high five as she said, "Now we need to hear what Kitty heard on that call."

"My thoughts exactly," I said. "And find that file!"

40

MR. BURGESS

As Kitty took the mirror from Abigail, she made a comment that caught everyone by surprise. "This mirror is part of a vanity set, yes. But it belongs to Nate. That package was addressed to the owner of this house."

Mandy said, "We owned the mirror, but then Mr. Burgess bought it from us."

"The tall guy with a walking stick and a British accent? Dressed in an old-fashioned suit?"

"Yes, him," Mandy said. "And he left the sketch and that number you called."

Kitty nodded. "About that man. Did you see him?"

"Well no, but my clerk Helen did. She described him to me in fact. What are you getting at? Did the law firm know who he was?"

"Yes they did. He lived in Lancaster, a city on the

Lune River in northwest England. It was a seafaring port. He was of modest wealth, owning several merchant ships that crossed between the colonies and Lancaster. His daughter married and moved to America."

Nate said, "Could someone please just stop and explain? Like to start, what is a vanity set?"

Mandy touched his arm. "A vanity set is an older term for grooming tools. That hand mirror is the one I took from this house to sell in my shop. It appears to be part of a set Paul Revere crafted in the 1770s for a young woman."

"I still don't get what it has to do with anything you all are talking about."

Jo joined the explanation. "Margaret Peabody was a young British bride and for her honeymoon the couple came to Boston to visit friends. The American Revolutionary War broke out and her husband joined a British regiment that arrived to fight. He was at the first battle, the one fought on the North Bridge. He died here in Concord. His last name was Peabody." As Jo took in the surrounding faces, she realized what she had just done. She'd shared the story that whispers in the cemetery inspired.

Everyone had turned to her, waiting. Oh my gosh what have I done Jo thought.

"How do you know all that?" Mandy asked.

"Ah ah…" Jo looked at Lillia, before saying. "It was something Lillia and I were researching, sort of…"

Lillia tried covering for her. "Did we hear something like that on the tour last night Grauntie?"

Grauntie saw the look Lillia shot her and said, "Yes I believe we heard something like that."

Charlie and Beth, along with Amy, came bursting in through the open front door. "Hey what's everyone doing here?" Beth asked.

41

LILLIA

I breathed a sigh of relief for Jo. I knew she wanted no one to know about her special ability. At least not yet.

Grauntie looked at me with skepticism. I mouthed the word *later* and she gave me the okay signal back before saying, "Well hello there. I see you've brought your bayonet along with you Charlie. Be careful. Don't stab anyone."

"So back to the phone call please Kitty. Is there a reward? We have three pieces together now," Flo said.

"Okay, first about the man who bought the mirror."

Betty said, "What does it matter about him, you have the mirror now. Tell us what they said about the reward."

Kitty continued. "I need to tell you something more about who Mr. Burgess was. He was Margaret Peabody's father. And yes, you are right Jo, she built this house to stay near where her husband breathed his last breath."

"Oh for goodness sake woman. You must have gotten your trans-Atlantic wires crossed. There's no way the same man who bought the mirror is the father of Margaret. He'd be long dead. Turned to dust. Way gone!" Betty said shaking her head.

Kitty simply said, "He is way gone as you call it. Mr. Burgess was lost at sea in 1776."

I watched the mouths of everyone in the room fall open. Everyone except Jo and me.

42

THE FOURTH PIECE

Kitty took a deep breath. "I can't believe I just said that. But that is what the man on the phone said. I left him a very detailed message last night. Explaining the mirror and the flyer the man left. How Flo, Betty and Meg reached out to Abigail who has the brush. And then how they found me with the comb."

"Who is the law firm then? Is this just a hoax?" Abigail said.

"Far from it. The firm has existed over three hundred years and was used by Margaret's father for his business. I know that sounds stupid, unbelievable, but it fits. I sent them my email and they are forwarding photographs and documents in the hopes they can settle this."

Nate was the first to say, "What do you mean settle it?"

"Apparently when James Burgess passed away, the portion of his estate that was to go to his daughter never did. The whole thing was mishandled and never finalized. It has been accumulating over many decades and the trail to anyone who might have had a claim against it disappeared. Let me tell you what they've figured out so far. If the handwriting on the flyer matches the records they have, the inheritance is ours."

"You're kidding! Wouldn't it go to all Margaret's heirs?" Flo said.

Betty hands flew up to the side of her head. "Good grief. That could be hundreds of people and we'd be buried out in Sleepy Hollow before it's all figured out!"

"No worries Betty. The flyer spelled out his wishes that it go to whoever owned the four silver vanity set pieces. That would be the ruling by a court. Handwritten will or something like that the lawyer said. If you have the original paper he left, they'll test the age of the paper and compare handwriting to his original signature on papers. Who's got that?"

Jo quickly said, "I do. It's in my room back home. And it is old paper and different looking writing and…"

"Great Jo. I think we are on the right track. I'll follow the law firm's directions about how to handle it. Now just to find the last piece," Kitty said.

"You mean it's ours if we find the nail file?" Mandy

shouted. "I have a feeling it's here in this house! Come on Nate, let's go pull up that For Sale sign."

"We'll all help look for it," Betty shouted. "Dang but if this isn't the most fun I've had in a long time." And she and Flo disappeared into one of the upstairs bedrooms.

Charlie was turning over the wooden rifle he held in his hand. "You mean a file like for your fingernails?"

43

LILLIA

Charlie unwrapped the duct tape from his wooden gun. I gasped when I saw what was being revealed.

"You've got to be kidding," Jo said as she almost choked.

I looked at her and we both started laughing hysterically.

"What's so funny Lillia?" Nate asked as he and Mandy walked back in carrying the For Sale sign.

Jo, laughing so hard as this point that tears were running down her face, pointed to what Charlie held up for everyone to see. Amy was running around him barking like crazy. The commotion brought Flo and Betty out to the top of the steps. Kitty and Abigail peeked around the corner of the kitchen door where they had headed to search.

In the middle of it all, stood my little brother holding up the silver handled nail file with the scrolling letter P engraved on it.

Flo shouted out. "Lordy would you look at that!"

Betty thrust her fist in the air as she let out another "Woot toot!"

"How on earth did you find that?" I asked.

Charlie, not sure why such a little thing had caused this reaction, said, "Beth and I were getting old clothes out of the house. We were upstairs looking in the boy's closet and we found like a secret little room. Amy was sniffing around it so we followed her. Don't you remember Lillia?"

"Right after you tried scaring us," Beth said, sticking her tongue out at Jo.

"The hideaway place! I remember now." I had been afraid my claustrophobia would kick in, so I didn't explore that tight little secret place with them. And Jo had gone back to the other bedroom and didn't even see it.

Jo said, "That last piece of the Paul Revere set must have been given to Anthony and he put it with his other treasures."

"And then he died young, so it was never found," I said.

"Wait a minute. What are you two talking about," Mandy asked.

We were saved from explaining by Charlie butting in and saying to Jo, "Paul Revere? What does he have to do with this?"

In the middle of all the exciting chaos Grauntie briefly explained that Revere was not only part of the revolution, but his career was as a silversmith.

Charlie stood with his mouth hanging slightly open. "So I duct taped something Paul Revere made to the end of a wooden rifle and used it as part of my Halloween costume? I can't wait to tell my history teacher back home. She'll never believe it."

Grauntie pulled out her phone. "Hold it up Charlie." She snapped a photograph. "There now. It's recorded for posterity. Go on with your story about finding it."

Still in awe Charlie said, "It was just there in the hideaway space. I had a dream that made me want to put it back to where I found it. I didn't mean to make trouble Mr. Conner."

Beth piped up. "Dad, you said we could use anything we wanted for costumes."

Nate pulled Charlie and Beth together in a big hug. "I did honey. Thank you Charlie for bringing it back though."

"You're welcome Mr. Conner. Can we go outside with Amy now?"

Grauntie stepped in and said, "Just for a few minutes Charlie. We'll be taking off soon to catch our flight out of Boston."

44

ALL TOGETHER

"All right Grauntie," Charlie shouted as he bounded out the door with Amy leaping ahead of him.

Nate and Mandy were examining the silver handled nail file. "How lucky is it that a curious boy found that secret hideaway?"

Jo was looking at them. "Does this mean you'll keep this house? You'll have money to fix it up?"

"I guess that depends on how much the Burgess Estate is worth. Kitty, you never said that. Is it enough to form a company with all of us and make this into a bed and breakfast?" Nate said.

"Oh it's enough. No problem there," Kitty replied. She hadn't explained to anyone that if the amount wouldn't have been enough, she would have invested in this project with her own money. She looked at the smiling faces around her. But this was so much better, now we all have a stake in it.

Meg and Jo were happy that the plan to restore the house was back on. Dad would get to see his dream turned into reality.

Abigail looked at her new friends. She was thankful for the twists and turns her life had taken in the past few days because now she was part of something. Her life would never be the same.

Mandy asked, "Kitty, how we will we connect to work together on the house? We all want you to be a part of the day-to-day stuff."

Meg suggested video chatting. But Kitty had a better idea. "Taking that flight to come here with the comb was only the beginning of being freer and more spontaneous. I've decided I'd like to rent a small place here while the work is being done."

"We've got the apartment above the workroom you can use," Nate said.

"Sounds perfect," Kitty replied.

"Well guess this calls off our big search. So happy for you all. And remember Flo and I will be available to run the place for you," Betty said. "We could be the two old ladies who add character to the joint."

Abigail said, "I would love to help with the decorating. Mandy, maybe I could work with you to find antiques to fill the place up?"

45

LILLIA

I tried to take in everything that had just happened. What a swirl!

Yesterday I was giving up.

Last night I was excited with renewed possibilities.

Today things fell into place. I felt happy for them all. And for the house that would now have a new life.

We all got and gave lots of hugs and promises to keep in touch. In fact, Kitty said we could use her house if we ever went to Apache Junction. She would be hanging out here in Concord for the next months.

"That sounds wonderful! I think I'll take you up on that. The winters in Kansas can be brutal," Grauntie said.

"I will have the pool man keep the water heated so you can enjoy it while you're there. And use my convertible all you want," Kitty said.

"Pool boy? Convertible? Sounds like you lead a nice life in Arizona!" Flo said. "Sure you want to spend the winter here in this cold?"

Kitty didn't hesitate to answer. "I know I do. Comfort is one thing, but so are fun and friends. Listen, how about someday we build a Peabody Bed & Breakfast in Arizona?"

Nate and Mandy had been standing to one side talking with Meg. Mandy raised her hand to get everyone's attention. "It appears that we, by the luck of owning this house, have one half of the pieces needed to claim the estate. Meg came up with a wonderful idea and Nate and I agree with her. We'd like to give this nail file to Flo and Betty because of their part in finding Abigail and her brush."

"Which led to Kitty and her comb. Without them, we wouldn't have been able to pull up the For Sale sign," Nate added.

Abigail clapped her hands. "Yes!"

Kitty nodded. "Perfect!"

Flo and Betty, for once, were speechless.

"Please say yes. Otherwise we'd have to pay you to run the place." Mandy said.

"It's a deal then," Flo said. "Okay, Betty Boo?"

"Okay!"

Nate and Mandy turned to me and Grauntie. "And

the doors will always be open to you."

Jo winked at me. I knew she'd keep my secret, and I'd keep hers.

And so on a quiet street in Concord, plans for the future blossomed. I knew the Peabody house would soon be full of life and fun and laughter again.

As we walked out toward our car Jo said to me, "You seeing Margaret in that mirror started all of this you know."

"You were the one that wrote the story," I said.

"Please, let's stay friends always."

"We will. I'll put Tiffany in touch with you, it that's okay. She's cool with all the paranormal stuff," I said.

Jo smiled. "I think I'd like that."

I hugged her goodbye one more time.

"Come on Charlie and Lillia. Car's loaded up and ready to go," Grauntie called.

And so, as a cool breeze sent the fall leaves skipping along Mill Street, we waved goodbye to new friends.

Funny how I started out looking for one thing and ended up finding so much more.

In the end, my brother Charlie and I both found what we were looking for in this quiet little town of Concord, Massachusetts.

. . .

The End

A MESSAGE FROM THE AUTHOR...

I hope you enjoyed *Whispering Graves*. It's the seventh book in my *Pameroy Mystery Series*. Each one will be set in a different state. I've got a lot of writing ahead of me... but I love it!

If you liked *Whispering Graves*, I would appreciate a review. Reviews help readers discover books and help me reach new audiences.

You can visit my website at www.pameroymystery.com for news and information. Be sure to check out photographs used as inspiration for in each book in the series. And you can sign up for my newsletter to learn when the next mystery will be published.

Happy reading... Brenda Felber

f facebook.com/brendafelberauthor

O instagram.com/brendafelber

P pinterest.com/bbfelber

a amazon.com/author/brendafelber

ALSO BY BRENDA FELBER

Unsettled Things, A Pameroy Mystery in Kentucky

Watched Places, A Pameroy Mystery in Alabama

Haunted Hills, A Pameroy Mystery in South Dakota

Locked Doors, A Pameroy Mystery in Wisconsin

Twisted Games, A Pameroy Mystery in North Carolina

Ghostly Tours, A Pameroy Mystery in Texas

Made in the
USA
Lexington, KY